# S.N.A.C.K.S.

## Speedy, Nutritious and Cheap Kids' Snacks

### Jan Brink and Melinda Ramm

*Illustrated by Roberta Simanowitz*

A PLUME BOOK

**NEW AMERICAN LIBRARY**

NEW YORK AND SCARBOROUGH, ONTARIO

PLUME TRADEMARK REG. U.S. PAT. OFF. AND FOREIGN COUNTRIES
REGISTERED TRADEMARK—MARCA REGISTRADA
HECHO EN WESTFORD, MASS., U.S.A.

SIGNET, SIGNET CLASSIC, MENTOR, PLUME, MERID-
IAN and NAL BOOKS are published *in the United States* by
New American Library, 1633 Broadway, New York, New
York 10019, *in Canada* by The New American Library of
Canada Limited, 81 Mack Avenue, Scarborough, Ontario
M1L 1M8.

LIBRARY OF CONGRESS CATALOGING IN PUBLICATION-DATA
Brink, Jan.
S.N.A.C.K.S.: speedy, nutritious, and cheap kids' snacks.
Includes index.
1. Snack foods.   2. Cookery (Natural foods)   I. Ramm,
Melinda.   II. Title.   III. Title: SNACKS.
TX740.B66   1984       641.5'55       83-26459
ISBN 0-452-25525-2

First Plume Printing, May, 1984

1 2 3 4 5 6 7 8 9

PRINTED IN THE UNITED STATES OF AMERICA

## WHEN APPLES OR RAISINS DON'T SEEM SPECIAL ENOUGH

Here are recipes for everything from creative treats like Spicy Popcorn and Banana Pom Poms to traditional favorites like Milkshakes, Brownies, Oatmeal Cookies, and Pizza—all natural and without added sugar or salt.

So don't panic if you're the soccer coach and have to provide half-time treats. Whip up something fast, tasty, inexpensive and nutritious. Your kids will taste the difference—and they'll love every bite.

## S.N.A.C.K.S.

### Speedy, Nutritious and Cheap Kids' Snacks

## ABOUT THE AUTHORS

JAN BRINK and MELINDA RAMM were neighbors trading recipes for nutritious Halloween treats when they hit upon the idea for S.N.A.C.K.S. Jan now lives in Washington, and Melinda lives in Connecticut. Their families have tested every recipe!

Mary Auer
Jim Brink
Carole Hall
Joan Gunderson Lyon
Carol Mann
Frank Martin
Joanne Michaels
H. David Ramm

*and special thanks to*

Todd Ramm,
who believed in *S.N.A.C.K.S.* as much as we did,
and more importantly believed in us.

Because we have always loved animals,
we intend to donate part of
the money we earn from *S.N.A.C.K.S.*
to help them.

# · Contents ·

# · Introduction ·

It's eight o'clock at night and your daughter says that tomorrow it's her turn to bring story-time snacks.

Your son's birthday party is coming up and he expects a bakery sheet cake.

As soccer coach, you have the honor of providing half-time treats for the next game.

Perhaps you've had an experience like one of these. They're situations that can throw nutrition-oriented parents into a tizzy!

What to do? Forget good nutrition and break down and buy junk?

One Halloween, a few years ago, we faced the challenge of "treating" a neighborhood full of ghosts and goblins. Junk food was out: we didn't believe in it, we didn't eat it, so we certainly couldn't serve it to trick-or-treaters. That's when the idea for S.N.A.C.K.S. was born. We realized every family needs recipes for wholesome, affordable, kid-pleasing treats to keep on hand for everyday snacking as well as for special occasions—recipes that contain no refined sugar, salt, white "enriched" flour, preservatives, and artificial flavors or colors.

Industrious, resourceful parents who work hard to ensure that their kids' meals are wholesome and balanced shouldn't be stymied when snack-time comes along. Between-meal treats can and should be a positive part of your child's diet. Quite simply,

1

snacks should be as good for your child as the rest of the food he eats.

We realize that "good for your child" is a nebulous phrase, at best. What we mean by it is that snacks should be consistent with the USDA's "Dietary Goals for Americans," the generally accepted criteria for good nutrition:

1. Eat a variety of foods.
2. Maintain an ideal weight.
3. Avoid too much fat, saturated fat, and cholesterol.
4. Eat foods with adequate starch and fiber.
5. Avoid too much sugar.
6. Avoid too much sodium.

We also believe children's snacks should be inexpensive, irresistibly tasty, and quick and easy to prepare. We believe that all the recipes in *S.N.A.C.K.S.* meet these standards. We hope you'll agree.

# · Speedy Snacks ·
## Quick Ways to Make Quality Treats

How you organize your kitchen, how you shop, and how you approach each recipe can greatly reduce the time it takes to make good snacks. In this section, we've listed lots of time-saving ideas we discovered while working on *S.N.A.C.K.S.* You may already be considerably better organized than we were when we started, so some of the basic things we've learned to do—like clearing lots of space on the counter before we start cooking—may seem obvious to you. But read on. There's bound to be a tip or two that could save you at least a few precious minutes.

### Sensible Storage

- Store your most-used equipment—bowls, utensils, pots and pans, muffin tins, and cookie sheets—within easy reach. Hang them on hooks or a pegboard whenever you can, so that you don't waste time getting them out.
- Keep equipment you seldom use (the hard-boiled egg slicer, for example) out of the way—in another room, another drawer, or in the back of the cabinet.
- Keep your herbs and spices on a Lazy Susan or in a spice rack. When our spices were stacked randomly in a cabinet,

not only were they difficult to get at quickly, we often didn't even know what we had!

- Store vanilla, cinnamon, nutmeg, baking powder, and baking soda together because they're so often used together.
- Store canned goods by category. (Keep canned fruits separate from the tuna, for example.)
- Set bottles of messy liquids such as oil, honey, and lecithin on large plastic container tops to save time cleaning the cabinets.
- Set aside a section of the refrigerator and a section of the cabinets for your children so that they can go by themselves to get snacks without having to interrupt you.
- Store vitamins where children *can't* get at them. This is one kind of health-builder that you don't want your kids to be able to reach.
- Chop nuts when you buy them, and store them chopped.
- Slice and wrap cheese before you freeze or refrigerate it. Slices are easier to use, and you don't have to thaw an entire block.
- Store nut butters upside down. This helps spread the oils more evenly throughout. Stir well with a knife before refrigerating.
- Keep a container of grated cheese in the refrigerator for use in recipes.
- Keep dried fruit in airtight but child-accessible containers.
- Keep some kind of fruit juice on hand at all times.
- Keep kid-sized portions of baked goods in the freezer.
- Wash fruits and vegetables before refrigerating them so that they can be grabbed by kids and eaten right away.

## Useful Equipment

*Blender*—the only small electrical appliance we consider a must. A blender is the fastest, easiest way to whirl fruits into juices and vegetables into soups, and to make batters, drinks, baby food, and practically anything else. If you keep your blender on the counter, you may find yourself using it daily.

*Candy thermometer*—the most accurate and reliable way to test candy when it is cooking. To use, put the thermometer in the candy mixture before starting to cook and leave it in during cooking. Be sure it is standing upright in the mixture and that the bulb is completely covered but not resting on the bottom or touching the side of the pan. Read the thermometer at eye level and watch the temperature closely. When the candy is done, remove the thermometer and allow it to cool before washing.

*Citrus peeler*—a hard, plastic gadget that cuts quickly through the rind, making it easy to turn the rind over and remove the fruit sections.

*Drip-free pitchers*—for pouring messy liquids like liquid lecithin, honey, and maple syrup. The pitchers with the sliding metal tops are worth the few cents more, as the one-piece plastic ones continue to drip after you've finished pouring.

*Food processor*—for doing many jobs quickly, easily, and neatly. Our recipes were timed without using one, but virtually all recipes take less time if you do. However, you can certainly get along without a processor if you have a sharp knife, a carving board, and a blender.

*Fruit wedger*—a gadget that both cores a fruit and makes wedges in one fell swoop. It makes kid-sized servings of apples and short work of pie-making. Buy the sturdier model, which is all in one piece; the lighter, hinged model is likely to fly apart when faced with its first solid Red Delicious.

*Honey bears*—those squeezable plastic, bear-shaped containers in which some honey is sold. These bears make handy no-spill containers that your kids will love to use. After the first "bearful" of honey is gone, just replenish it with the honey from a more economical jar.

*Muffin tins*—for making any cake or quick-bread recipe both portable and kid-sized. Divide the batter into muffin tins and make a double batch so you can freeze some for future instant treats.

*Paper cups*—can be used for much more than just disposable juice servers. They can become popsicle molds merely by adding a stick. They also make great bowls for your toddler's portable snacks.

*Popsicle molds*—for making yogurt and juice pops as well as ices, ice creams, and frozen puddings. Yes, a paper cup will do the job, but molds are both easier and neater. Ours are in use all summer long.

*Serrated bread knife*—to avoid shredding loaves of bread. As you begin to bake your own breads or buy whole-grain solid loaves, you'll find you use one all the time.

**Swizzles**—to serve just the right amount of honey or syrup. We like the plastic ones better than the wooden ones. They clean more easily, dry more quickly, and don't absorb the honey.

**Wire whisks**—the cheapest egg beaters around. Gourmet cooks swear by them. We find them handy, especially for the "wet" half of many of our recipes. A whisk can also be used to mix and lighten dry ingredients instead of having to sift them. A medium-sized one, about ten inches long, is a good size to start with.

**Yogurt maker**—if you eat and serve lots of yogurt. Yogurt makers can be a big help; however, you can make yogurt without one, and we show you how on page 16.

## Simplified Shopping

- Keep a running grocery list on your refrigerator. It works alot better than telling yourself, "I'll surely remember to buy _____." Then make a final list before you go, in the order in which items are stocked in the store.
- Do careful label-reading (see page 10) once and remember which brands are acceptable so you can head right to them each time you shop.
- Look for products with short lists of ingredients. Generally speaking, highly adulterated products have longer lists of ingredients than unadulterated versions of the same products. This trick doesn't work all the time, but it works often enough to save you time by keeping it in mind.
- Avoid junk food rows. If you must go down them at all, don't even glance at "Cheese Whamos"!
- Take along a wholesome snack for any children shopping with you. A portable snack will help cut down on constant "gimmes" and make shopping more pleasant for both you and the kids.
- While unloading your grocery cart at the store, try to keep like items together. If you unload all the frozen items at the same time, or all the canned goods together at the checkout counter, you'll speed the chore of unloading when you get home.

## Quicker Cooking

The time shown for each recipe in *S.N.A.C.K.S.* is the length of time it takes us to prepare it to be baked or refrigerated after we have cleared a work area on the counter and gotten out all ingredients and utensils.

All our recipes require less than 15 minutes *advance* preparation. The preparation time, which appears on all recipes, does not include cooking time or refrigeration time.

Here are some tricks we've learned to keep preparation time to a minimum:

- Read each recipe with an eye to saving time. Do you really need four steps, or can it be done in two? Do you have to cut paper-thin slices or will chunks work? (To chunk citrus fruit, peel, seed, and break it into small pieces that can readily be used. To chunk other fruits and vegetables, scrub, peel if necessary, core or pit, then cube or coarsely slice them.)
- Learn to "eyeball" your measurements. They seldom have to be exact. Remember, you are not cooking for gourmets. About the only ingredient where too much can be a disaster is salt, and since we don't use it in our recipes, you don't have to worry about it.
- Use the fewest number of utensils possible. When you can, mix in one bowl instead of two. Use only the blender, not the blender and a mixing bowl. Instead of using all your measuring cups, use only the largest and approximate the amount.
- Make double batches, serving half and saving half. The second half of any recipe, no matter how time-consuming it was to make in the first place, becomes a quick treat when you just have to take it out of the freezer.
- Prop up your recipe book or card as close to eye level as possible, so that you can see it at a glance.
- Use your blender or processor whenever you can, even if the recipe doesn't call for one. Dry ingredients, as well as wet, can be combined in either. A processor can often substitute for a mixer, mixing bowl, cutting board and knife, and more.
- Consider using your baking pan as a mixing bowl. Start with the oil in the recipe, swish it around the pan, add and combine the rest of the wet ingredients, then add the dry ingredients. Or grease the pan first, add wet ingredients, then dry, and

mix. This method skips the mixing bowl step altogether.

- Don't sift flour—whisk it instead.
- When a recipe calls for both honey and oil, measure the oil first, then add the honey to the same measuring cup. The honey will slide right out of the oiled cup.
- "Grease" with liquid lecithin—and things will slide right out of pans or off cookie sheets. Drizzle a pencil-thin criss-cross of lecithin on the bottom of the pan. A little goes a long way; about ½ teaspoon is enough for a cookie sheet. Pop it into the preheating oven for a minute, then spread the lecithin with a piece of paper towel.
- Give some thought to other ways you can save time by asking yourself, "Are there ways in which I could make this easier? Am I making more work for myself?" You may discover that the way you've always done something is not necessarily the quickest. Think fast!

# · Nutritious Snacks ·

## Kids *Are* What You Feed Them

If "you are what you eat," then it stands to reason that your children are what you feed them. The examples you set for them and the eating patterns you establish in their childhood will help develop their lifelong eating habits and attitudes toward foods. One pop-tart might not be dangerous, but a lifetime of sugared and salted foods is.

That's why it's so important that the foods you buy and prepare—the foods with your "stamp of approval"—be as pure and nutritious as possible. For example, even if you never manage to eliminate refined sugar completely, just cutting back on it is a step in the right direction for your kids. The more nutritious the foods you bring home are, the higher the quality of the snacks you can provide. When your kitchen is stocked with wholesome foods, there is no end to the snacks you can whip up—or simply grab —without having to rely on processed junk foods.

A quick look at the foods already in your kitchen will probably reveal some—or many—that contain chemicals, dyes, and preservatives. There are two basic approaches you can take to this: you can pitch them, which, though preferable, is not really practical, or you can use them and replace them with less adulterated and more wholesome foods. The latter is a more sensible approach, and one your kids are less likely to notice or resent.

9

## Buy the Right Foods

Here are a few hints to help you choose the most beneficial foods possible:

- Remember this basic rule of thumb: fresh is best, frozen is next, and canned is usually a poor third.
- Buy whole foods. Make farmers, not chemists, the source of food for your family. Buy unprocessed foods and avoid additives. Choose pure products rather than imitations.
- Eliminate refined white cane sugar, brown sugar, and "raw turbinado" sugar. Today sugar is in the oddest things—soups, catsup, seafood, mayonnaise, even pizzas.
- Read the labels right in the store; if the list of ingredients includes sugar in any form (dextrose, fructose, glucose, lactose, maltose, or sucrose), put it back.
- Decrease the amount of saturated fats in the foods you buy for your family. Here are some sensible ways to cut down:
- Choose low-fat protein sources like chicken, fish, and legumes instead of red meats.
- Read food labels, avoiding those foods that list "saturated" or "vegetable fat," "hydrogenated" fat or oil, or "hardened" fat or oil on the label.
- Do not buy products made from coconut or palm oils.
- Choose mayonnaise and salad dressings made from unsaturated oils.
- Buy the least fatty dairy products your kids will tolerate. There is as much nutrition in skim milk as there is in whole, but without the butterfat; thus, skim milk is a better choice than low-fat milk, and low-fat a better choice than whole milk. Avoid butter and hydrogenated margarine; use Butter's Brother instead (see page 14), or choose margarines that list liquid vegetable oil first.
- Buy pure, unhydrogenated peanut butter, or make your own (see page 16).
- Look for salt-free and salt-reduced products, and choose them when you have the option.
- Choose slow-cooking hot cereals instead of instant. Since all types of hot cereals are easy to prepare, the time you save with the instant doesn't make up for the nutrition you lose.

- Brown rice is the best nutritional choice, converted white next, and "instant rice" should be a last, desperation choice only.
- Choose your flour carefully. "Enriched" and "refined" flours are pretty and white, but practically useless as a food. Use whole wheat or unbleached flour. We use each, sometimes interchangeably. Whole wheat flour has a stronger taste and heavier texture than unbleached. If you want to use whole wheat flour but are uneasy about your children's acceptance of it, start out by using equal parts of unbleached and whole wheat flour. As they become more accustomed to it, increase the ratio of whole wheat to unbleached.
- Buy sparkling water rather than highly salted club soda.
- Select unsweetened fruit juices.
- When buying canned fruits, pick those packed in juice not syrup.
- Buy polyunsaturated vegetable oils which are liquid at room temperature. These include safflower oil, corn oil, soy oil, sunflower oil, or a combination of them.
- Buy plain yogurt and make your own flavored yogurt by adding fruits, jams, or juice concentrates.
- Labels reading "Made with honey" or "Made with carob" don't necessarily mean that all ingredients in the product are health-building, as they may contain sugar and additives as well.
- Choose pure extracts instead of imitation flavorings.
- Look for pure maple syrup.

## Convert Old Recipes

Once your kitchen is stocked with the most nutritious ingredients possible, it's easy to convert your old recipes into good-for-your-children treats. It's a simple matter of experimenting. The following is a list of some of the tricks we use most often. A word of caution: they don't all work in every recipe. In time, though, you'll learn what will work, the exact proportions to use, and what your kids will accept.

- Substitute honey for sugar by using about ⅔ cup of honey for each cup of sugar called for. You may want to either decrease the amount of other liquids used or slightly increase the amount of flour called for, though you won't usually have to bother. Honey is primarily sugars—75-80 percent—but is easier to digest than cane or beet sugar. It has seven B vitamins, vitamin C, and traces of amino acids. Baked goods made with honey stay fresher and moister longer, as the honey retains moisture to help slow the drying process. Honey won't go bad. If it should crystalize, however, just place the jar in a pan of warm water until it is smooth and liquid again.

Even with all its benefits, honey is still a concentrated sweet, high in calories and carbohydrates, and shouldn't be poured in and on everything. If there is a blood sugar problem in your family, you would be wise to be as careful about honey as you are about sugar. One way of being careful is to not serve sweetened snacks alone between meals. Instead, serve them with milk or other proteins, or as desserts after a meal. This will help lessen the quick rise and subsequent drop in blood sugar levels that sweets can produce.

Recent studies suggest that honey can cause problems in infants and should therefore not be given to babies under a year old. The very young don't need sweetener in their diets, as they already get plenty of sugars from their milk, fruits, and vegetables. Check with your pediatrician if in doubt.

- Eliminate salt.
- Add bran or wheat germ to flour when baking. Use ¼ cup of each to 1½ cups of flour to get a flour mixture of 2 cups. Wheat germ is the embryo or "germ" located in the center of the wheat kernel. It is a good source of protein, B vitamins, potassium, and phosphorus. You can buy either raw or toasted wheat germ. Toasting it makes it more palatable and not as perishable but destroys some of its food value.
- Use milk instead of water.
- To increase the protein content of a recipe, add an egg, dried milk, cheese, or nuts and seeds.
- Use carob powder or our Super Syrup (see page 15) instead of chocolate.
- Omit food colorings or make your own (see page 17).
- Substitute chopped nuts or dried fruits for candy "spangles."
- Fruits and vegetables don't need to be peeled unless the skin is inedible or waxed.
- Make real whipped cream instead of using an artificial topping.

- Add granulated lecithin to dairy products, cereals, and baked goods. Lecithin is a polyunsaturated fat that works to break down blood fats. It helps the liver use fats properly, helps prevent fats from accumulating in the bloodstream, and helps the body absorb vitamins A and D. Lecithin has two important B vitamins, cholin and inositol, which should be in generous supply in any diet that contains saturated fats. Lecithin is found naturally in vegetable oils, egg yolk, and soybeans. In granulated form, lecithin can be added to baked goods, drinks, and cereals, among other things. It's good insurance for kids who may get too much saturated fat from processed foods, meats, and dairy products, and not enough vegetable oil.
- Choose low-fat ingredients when you can—skim milk instead of whole, or yogurt instead of sour cream, for example.
- When possible, use fresh ingredients instead of dried.
- Add molasses to recipes to increase iron.
- Reduce the cooking time of fruits and vegetables and steam them instead of boiling.
- Make crumb toppings of wheat germ, vegetable oil, and honey.
- For flavoring, use the whole food instead of bottled extracts—fresh lemons or almonds, for example.
- Broil or bake foods instead of frying.
- Use vegetable oil in foods eaten daily.
- Do not use shortening. Instead, use liquid lecithin or vegetable oil for greasing pans and polyunsaturated vegetable oil or Butter's Brother (see page 14) in cooking.
- Use vegetable oil or Butter's Brother instead of butter.
- Substitute Yogurt Cream Cheese (see page 163) for ordinary cream cheese.

## Rely on Homemade Basics
### BUTTER'S BROTHER

Margarine is loaded with added chemicals, preservatives, emulsifiers, and artificial colors. Butter does not have preservatives or emulsifiers, but it may contain artificial color and is a saturated fat. Except for sweet butter, both butter and margarine contain salt, an unnecessary additive in a small person's diet.

Better than either butter or margarine is Butter's Brother, which has half the saturated fat of butter and adds both polyunsaturated vegetable oil and lecithin to your children's diets.

## • BUTTER'S BROTHER •

1 cup vegetable oil
1 cup sweet butter, softened

2 tablespoons granulated lecithin

Mix all ingredients in a blender or processor until smoothly blended. Pour into a plastic container and chill.

## SUPER SYRUP

Chocolate is high in both calories and fat; nearly half of cocoa is fat. Chocolate also has a substance called oxalic acid which acts to prevent the body from absorbing calcium. (So much for the benefits of chocolate milk!) Carob doesn't taste just like chocolate, but we've provided you with recipes with carob that are so delicious they're bound to win over even the most diehard "chocoholics" in your family. Carob is naturally sweet, has plenty of B vitamins and minerals, and actually adds calcium. When compared to chocolate, carob has more than twice the calcium, half the calories, and 1/100th the fat.

Carob is usually sold as a powder, sometimes called carob flour. It is the dark brown powder produced from grinding the dried carob fruit itself. In a recipe, carob can either be used "as is" in chips or made into a syrup.

## • SUPER SYRUP •

| | |
|---|---|
| **1 cup carob powder** | **½ cup honey** |
| **1 cup water** | |

In a small saucepan, mix ingredients and bring to a boil over low heat. Cook gently, stirring occasionally, for 10 minutes. Chill and store in the refrigerator.

## REAL PEANUT BUTTER

The peanut butter in most of the popular brands on the market today is a hydrogenated fat, although peanuts and peanut oil are not. After the injury of turning kids' all-time favorite food into a saturated fat, the insult is added by including sugar, preservatives, and stabilizers.

You can still have good peanut butter on hand for your kids by either making it yourself or buying the right kind. Every health food store and most grocery stores sell a natural peanut butter which contains nothing more than ground peanuts. Taste and consistency vary greatly from brand to brand, though all will be more solid than the popular commercial brands. After opening the jar, you'll need to stir vigorously to distribute the oils and should store the jar in the refrigerator. If this natural peanut butter is too thick for your children's tastes, or if they're too young for a food this dense, you can thin it by mashing it with milk, yogurt, or cottage or ricotta cheese before serving.

Real peanut butter is easy to make at home.

## • REAL PEANUT BUTTER •

**2 cups peanuts**                                    **¼ cup vegetable oil**

Grind peanuts in a blender or processor about one minute, or until finely ground. Gradually add oil, about 1 tablespoon at a time, while continuing to process. Store in the refrigerator.

## HOMEMADE YOGURT

Yogurt is one of the best all-around foods you can serve children, including babies. When made with skim milk, it is low in both fat and calories and high in protein and B vitamins.

When buying yogurt, be careful that it doesn't contain gums, artificial color, flavor, or preservatives. Watch out for high amounts of sugar, either added to flavored yogurts or as an ingredient in the fruit jams.

## • HOMEMADE YOGURT •
### 10 minutes    4 cups

**4 cups milk**                                    **¼ cup plain yogurt**

Scald milk in a saucepan, then cool to room temperature. Add yogurt and stir well. (Blend in ¼ cup of dry milk powder, if desired, to increase protein and enhance creaminess.)

Pour mixture into a pre-warmed quart jar or glass bowl. Cover and wrap in a towel and place in a warm (115-118°F.) spot. If you have a gas oven, set it at 200°F. for 5 minutes. Turn it off and place yogurt inside. The pilot light will keep it warm.

Another idea is to fill an electric frying pan with hot water and set the temperature at 100°F. Place yogurt-filled container in water and cover pan.

Yogurt must sit undisturbed for 6-8 hours. Refrigerate when firm.

Reserve about ½ cup of yogurt to use as a starter for the next batch.

## FOOD COLORINGS

Kids love tinted frostings. You might think it is a lot of bother to make your own food coloring, but the following recipes are quite simple and they will keep in the refrigerator for days. You will need only a drop or two at a time. Colorings can be frozen for even longer storage. The most important thing about them, however, is that they are perfectly safe for your children.

### • BLUE •
6 minutes   1½ cups

**½ cup water**                               **½ cup blueberries**

Boil water and berries together for about 5 minutes. Strain and discard everything but the liquid. Store in a clean jar.

### • BROWN •
1 minute

Carob powder or syrup can be used to color and flavor frosting.

## • GREEN •
6 minutes    1 cup

**Spinach leaves or alfalfa tea**                    **½ cup water**

Boil spinach or tea and water for about 5 minutes. Strain and discard everything but liquid. Refrigerate in a clean jar.

## • ORANGE •
3 minutes    ¼ cup

**1 carrot**                              **¼ cup water**

Place carrot in a blender or food processor and process until it is ground into small pieces. Add water and continue to blend until mixture is smooth. Strain and store liquid in a clean jar.

## • PINK •

In place of the liquid called for in a frosting recipe, use cranberry juice. It adds a delicious flavor as it tints.

## • RED •
7 minutes    1 cup

**2 fresh beets, washed**                    **¾ cup water**

Place ingredients into a saucepan. Bring mixture to a boil and continue boiling for 5 minutes. Strain and discard everything but the liquid. Store in a clean jar. Use sparingly, as icing will pick up a little of the beet flavor.

## • YELLOW •
6 minutes   1 cup

**1 teaspoon saffron**                    **1 cup water**

Add saffron to boiling water and continue boiling 5 minutes. Allow mixture to cool; strain and pour liquid into a clean jar to store.

## • PEACH •

Mix 1 part Red Coloring to 1 part Yellow Coloring.

## • MAYONNAISE •
5 minutes   1½ cups

To make mayonnaise, we recommend using a blender or food processor. If you use a blender, remember to scrape down the sides repeatedly.

**2 tablespoons cider vinegar**           **½ teaspoon dry mustard**
**1 egg**                                 **1¼ cups vegetable oil**

Blend the first 3 ingredients about 1 minute.
    Continue blending and add oil in a slow and steady stream. Beat until oil is thoroughly blended.
    Store in a covered container and refrigerate.

## • BUSY BAKEQUICK •

Busy Bakequick is as versatile as the well-known commercial product.

It is a snap to make and use, and the resulting biscuits, cakes, muffins, pancakes, and waffles are sure kid-pleasers.

The following quantities can be doubled and even tripled if you'd like. The more you keep on hand, the more fast baking you'll find yourself doing.

**3⅓ cups unbleached flour**          **1⅔ tablespoons baking powder**

Whisk flour in a bowl. Add baking powder and continue to whisk until ingredients are combined.

Place in an airtight container and store in the refrigerator or freezer.

The following *S.N.A.C.K.S.* recipes use Bakequick:

# · Cheap Snacks ·
## How to Get Top Value for Your Money

High-quality snacks—foods that add to health rather than take away from it—are a wise expenditure of your food dollar. One less doctor bill for a child is worth far more than the difference between the cost of snacks that build health and snacks that help destroy it. Foods that will help a growing body to become as strong and resistant to illness as possible can be an added source of peace of mind for you. Can you really put a price on the health of your children?

Buying wholesome foods may mean that you will begin to do some of your shopping in health food stores. However, you can still do the majority of your shopping at the local supermarket. Here are some ideas that may help:

- The more processed the food, the more expensive it is likely to be. Consider the potato. Fresh, it costs practically nothing, but if you have someone else bake it, stuff it, add chemicals, put it in a spiffy aluminum jacket, freeze it, put it in a fancy box, and toss in an advertising budget, you end up with a very expensive vegetable indeed.
- Sometimes cheaper alternatives are also better for your children. Here are some double bonuses: fresh fruits and vegetables are cheaper and more healthful than canned or frozen ones, whole grains are cheaper and more healthful than most

21

red meats, homemade milkshakes are cheaper and more healthful than "instant breakfasts," old-fashioned cooked cereals are cheaper and more healthful than "instant cereals."

- Belonging to a food co-op can save you a lot of money. Buying in bulk directly from wholesalers enables co-ops to pass on the savings to their members.
- Certain foods are a better buy when purchased in bulk. These include rice, bran, flours, nuts, seeds, and cheeses. For example, you'll pay a lot less per ounce for peanuts if you buy a 10-pound bag instead of an 8-ounce jar. The disadvantages of this money-saver is that big bags and large jars are clumsy to work with. To get around this problem, keep a small jar filled with whatever is in those large bags or jars. Place the small jar somewhere where it can be used easily, preferably in the door of the freezer or refrigerator. This prevents you from wrestling with a 5-pound bag of sunflower seeds to get 2 tablespoons to sprinkle on yogurt.
- Buy and cook with fresh fruits and vegetables that are in season. Try shopping at roadside produce stands.
- Use less meat than the recipe calls for.
- Substitute powdered milk for regular.

Finally, you'll save money by saving energy in the kitchen. Keep the time the oven preheats to a minimum; some dishes, especially those that bake for a long time, don't even require a preheated oven. When possible, use the burners on the range instead of the oven. Also, use the smallest appliance necessary, for instance, the toaster instead of the broiler.

# · Absolutely Instant ·

Absolutely instant snacks are the simplest. They may even be the best. They can be handed to hungry youngsters on a minute's notice with virtually no preparation time, and they are loaded with nutrients that are a plus to kids' diets.

*Bread fingers:* quick and yeast breads cut into easy-to-manage strips.
*Cheese cubes*
*Crackers*
*Fruit:* canned, unsweetened (a good storage idea is to keep unopened cans on hand in the refrigerator); citrus smiles (grapefruit, orange, pineapple, tangerine segments); dried fruit (apples, apricots, banana chips, currants, figs, pineapple, prunes, and raisins); fresh fruit (apples, bananas, berries, cantaloupe, cherries, grapes, honeydew melon, peaches, pears, plums, watermelon, to name but a few)
*Juice:* fruit or vegetable (fresh or canned)
*Milk*
*Nuts:* almonds, cashews, peanuts, pecans, or walnuts by the handful or cup
*Peanut butter on a spoon*
*Seeds:* pumpkin, sesame, or sunflower seeds by the handful or cup
*Water:* seldom thought of, but sometimes this is all it takes

*Yogurt:* plain or sweetened with honey; add fruit and/or nuts, if desired

*Vegetables:* broccoli, carrots, cauliflower, celery, cherry tomatoes, cucumber, green beans, lettuce, mushrooms, olives, pepper rings, raw potato chunks, radishes, squash, tomatoes, zucchini

# · Kid-Do-Able ·

Cooking can be a creative outlet. Most children enjoy participating, especially if they are making something they like. Older children may want to try their hand at making some of their own snacks. Younger ones like to watch and help.

Many of the recipes in *S.N.A.C.K.S.* are "kid-do-able"—that is, children can make them with little or no parental help. How much supervision is needed obviously depends on the age, maturity, and ability of the child. Each of you knows your own children best, and you should decide if they are capable of handling certain foods—or using appliances and utensils that could be dangerous if not wielded properly.

We think the following recipes are the easiest and safest for kids to make themselves.

### • AMBROSIA •
5 minutes   Serves 6

A heavenly taste!

| | |
|---|---|
| **2 cups grated carrots** | **½ cup shredded coconut** |
| **1 cup crushed pineapple,** | **½ cup raisins** |
| **drained** | **Plain yogurt (optional)** |

Mix all ingredients together and serve immediately or chill in the refrigerator. Serve with yogurt, if desired.

### • APPLE–PEANUT RAISIN GOODIES •
5 minutes   Serves 4

**1 apple**                                                              **Raisins**
**Peanut butter**

Cut the apple into 8 slices and remove the core.

Spread one side of each slice with about 1 teaspoon of peanut butter and sprinkle with about 1 teaspoon of raisins. Serve immediately or store in the refrigerator.

## • NO-COOK CANDIED APPLES •
### 5 minutes

**For each serving:**

**1 apple**
**Honey**

**Shredded coconut, gorp (see page 38 for our version), granola, chopped nuts, or sesame seeds**

Insert a wooden popsicle stick into each apple. Dip the apple into honey and allow the excess to drip off. Roll the honey-covered apple in one of the remaining ingredients. Serve immediately or set on waxed paper and store in the refrigerator for several days.

## • PEANUT BUTTER BANANAS •
### 5 minutes   Serves 2

**2 ripe bananas**
**½ cup peanut butter**
**⅓ cup orange juice**

**¾ cup shredded coconut or finely chopped peanuts**

Peel and slice bananas in half lengthwise.

Spread each half with peanut butter and put slices back together to form sandwiches. Brush with orange juice and roll in shredded coconut or chopped peanuts.

Cut into 1-inch pieces and serve as a snack or use to garnish fresh fruit salad.

Store in the refrigerator or freezer.

## • BRANOLA CEREAL SNACK •
5 minutes    Serves 2

Double or triple this recipe to make a larger batch and use as an anytime-snack. Store in an airtight container.

6 tablespoons bran
2 tablespoons raisins
4 teaspoons sunflower seeds

2 teaspoons wheat germ
⅔ cup milk

Combine the first 4 ingredients in a bowl. Pour milk over the mixture and allow it to soak before serving.

## • CHEWY NUT BARS •
5 minutes    2½ dozen

2 cups peanuts or sunflower
    seeds
5 tablespoons honey

1 tablespoon molasses
Raisins, carob powder, or
    sesame seeds (optional)

Grind nuts or seeds to the consistency of flour; a blender or food processor works best. Stir in honey and molasses. If you want, add some raisins or seeds to mixture before pressing it into a greased baking pan. Or after patting mixture into a pan, sprinkle with carob powder and sesame seeds. Chill mixture and cut into squares.

Store in an airtight container and refrigerate or freeze.

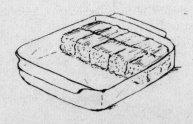

## • DATE NUTS •
5 minutes   2 dozen

Pecans and walnuts are good choices to use.

**1 cup dates, chunked**
**¼-½ cup raisins**
**1 cup nuts**

**Shredded unsweetened coconut**

Combine the first 3 ingredients in a blender or food processor until they are finely ground and blended. Form small balls by rolling the mixture between your palms. Roll balls in shredded coconut. Serve immediately.

Store in an airtight container and refrigerate.

## • STUFFED DATES •
5 minutes

Very sweet and rich tasting! One or two will be enough for anyone. The variety of stuffings and coatings that can be used make this snack a real kid-pleaser.

Pit dates.

Stuff each date with: mashed banana, cream cheese, fruit butter, honey butter, peanut butter, ricotta cheese or any combination of these foods.

Roll stuffed dates in: shredded coconut, honey, chopped nuts, seeds, or wheat germ.

For the pièce de résistance, top with a favorite nut: almond, peanut, pecan, or walnut.

Store in an airtight container and refrigerate.

## • FRUIT DUNK •
5 minutes    Serves 2

The beauty of this snack is that it is easy to take along when you are traveling. Simply put precut fruit in a plastic bag and let children dunk fruit into a container of yogurt whenever they are hungry. It can also be dressed up and served to company by putting the yogurt and fruit on a pretty serving dish, arranging the fruit in an attractive fashion. Simple or fancy, no one will dispute how good it tastes.

**1 cup plain yogurt**                    **1 pear, cored and sliced**
**1 apple, cored and sliced**

Stir yogurt until well mixed. Dunk and enjoy.

*Variation:*
   Use any other fruits that your children prefer.
   Plain yogurt can be sweetened to taste with honey if it is too tart.

## • GRANOLA SPLIT •
5 minutes

**For each serving:**

**1 banana, peeled and cut in**          **Granola**
   **half lengthwise**                    **Raisins**
**½ cup cottage cheese, ricotta**        **Chopped nuts**
   **cheese or plain yogurt**

Spoon cheese or yogurt on top of banana halves. Sprinkle with granola, raisins, and nuts. Serve immediately.

*Variations:*
   Substitute peaches for the bananas.
   Substitute gorp for the granola.
   Spoon 1 tablespoon of either fresh or frozen pineapple juice or orange juice concentrate over the split. Some other fruit ideas include: chunked apples mixed with yogurt, or blueberries, crushed pineapple, or strawberries.

## • ICE CREAM BALLS •
3 minutes

**For each serving:**

   Scoop out a ball of ice cream (about 1 cup) using an ice cream scoop or a large spoon.
   Roll each ball in one of the following: applesauce, crushed berries, shredded coconut, chopped fruit, fruit butters, gorp, granola, chopped nuts, or crushed pineapple.
   Top with whipped cream, sliced fruit, sour cream, or plain yogurt if desired.
   Serve immediately or place in freezer.

## • ICE CREAM SANDWICHES •
2 minutes

**For each serving:**

**1 tablespoon ice cream,**               **2 graham crackers**
   **slightly softened**

Spread ice cream carefully on one cracker. Top with remaining cracker and serve immediately. Place in freezer, if desired, and serve later.

*Variations:*

Substitute your children's favorite cookies for the graham crackers.

Sandwich ice cream between 2 thin slices of cake. Serve immediately or freeze.

## • ICE CREAM SUNDAES •
### 5 minutes

Make your own ice cream sundaes using our recipes and fresh wholesome ingredients.

### Ice Cream

| | |
|---|---|
| Strawberry Ice Cream | (page 155) |
| Tutti-Frutti Ice Cream | (page 155) |
| Vanilla Ice Cream | (page 156) |
| Walnut Ice Cream | (page 156) |

### Toppings

hot applesauce
cranberry sauce
mixed fresh fruit
fruit butters
warm honey

warm maple syrup
peanut butter or other nut
  butters
Super Syrup (page 15)

### Garnishes

shredded coconut
whipped cream
chopped fruit
gorp

granola
chopped nuts
seeds

## • KIDDIE CANDY •
5 minutes   2 dozen

**1 cup peanut butter**         **1½ cups noninstant dry milk**
**1 cup honey**

In a shallow pan, mix peanut butter and honey until blended. Stir in dry milk and mix well. Spread mixture evenly in pan and chill until firm.

To serve: cut candy into squares or remove from pan and roll into balls.

Store in a covered container in the refrigerator.

*Variations:*

Add ½ cup of carob powder to mixture before chilling.

Add 1 cup of wheat germ or rolled oats and blend well.

## • MELLOW YELLOWS •
5 minutes

Mighty appealing served at breakfast or as a quick luncheon salad as well as a fast snack.

Peel and divide into sections or slices one or more of these fruits: grapefruit, oranges, pineapple, or tangerines.

Dip citrus slices in honey or partially thawed frozen juice concentrate; then in plain or toasted shredded coconut. Serve immediately or place in the freezer to serve later.

## • PEANUT-RAISIN GRAHAMS •
2 minutes

These are quick to make, easy to take along, and are super tasting. Who could ask for more in a snack? Try using the Graham Scram Cookies on page 94.

**For each serving:**

**2 graham crackers**                     **2 teaspoons raisins**
**1 tablespoon peanut butter**

Carefully spread 1 graham cracker with peanut butter and sprinkle with raisins. Top with the other cracker.

If this is too much for your little one to eat, use 1 graham cracker broken into 2 pieces.

## • PRESTO PUMPKIN PUDDING •
5 minutes   Serves 6

**2 cups pumpkin puree**               **2 teaspoons honey**
**2 eggs**                             **½ banana, peeled and sliced**
**½ teaspoon cinnamon**

Blend all the ingredients until mixture is smooth and thoroughly blended. Serve immediately or store in the refrigerator. It may also be frozen to make Pudding-on-a-Stick (page 41).

*Variations:*
    Add a little wheat germ or bran to thicken pudding.
    Sprinkle chopped nuts, seeds, shredded coconut, granola, or a slice of banana on top of pudding.
    For a more refreshing, thicker pudding, add a chunked *frozen* banana.

## • RAINBOW PARFAIT •
### 5 minutes

Use your imagination to make this lovely, light dessert look as stunning as it tastes.

**For each serving:**

Layer ricotta cheese (about ½-1 cup) in a parfait glass with about 1 cup of your children's favorite fruits. Some good ideas are: chunked apples, bananas, berries (blueberries, raspberries, and strawberries), grapes, melon, peaches, or pineapple.

Serve chilled and, if desired, topped with gorp, granola, nuts, seeds, or raisins.

*Variations:*
Substitute cottage cheese for ricotta cheese.
Add a mashed banana and blend in with the cheese.

## • RICE YOGURT •
### 5 minutes   Serves 2

A great anytime snack for when the kids get tired of sandwiches.

¾ cup cooked brown rice
¼-⅓ cup plain yogurt
2 tablespoons raisins

1 tablespoon chopped nuts
Dash of cinnamon

In a small bowl, stir all the ingredients until blended. Serve immediately or chill in the refrigerator.

*Variation:*
Add 1-2 tablespoons of chopped apple and ½ teaspoon of honey.

## • SUMMER SUNDAE SAUCE •
5 minutes    Serves 2

**1 cup cottage or ricotta**                    **1 tablespoon honey**
**cheese or Yogurt Cream**
**Cheese (page 163)**

Blend cheese or yogurt with honey.
   Stir in *one* of the following spices:
                ¼ teaspoon allspice
                ½ teaspoon cinnamon
                ½ teaspoon nutmeg
   Spoon cheese sauce over chilled orange sections, strawberries, or whatever fruit you prefer. Serve immediately or store covered in the refrigerator.

## • ALMOST CHOCOLATE SODA •
2 minutes

**For each serving:**

Spoon 2 or 3 tablespoons of Super Syrup (page 15) into a glass. Add natural sparkling water and stir until drink is well blended and frothy. Serve immediately.

## • NATURAL FRUIT SODA •
2 minutes

**For each serving:**

**¼ cup apple, grape, or orange juice**     **Natural sparkling water**
     **or**
**2 tablespoons frozen fruit juice
   concentrate, thawed**

Put fruit juice or concentrate into a glass and add natural sparkling water. Stir well, add ice, and you have a real fruit soda.
    Any kind of juice or concentrate can be used, although you
may want to sweeten some by adding a little honey.

## • ORANGEADE •
2 minutes    Serves 2

**2 cups water**                 **3 tablespoons lemon juice**
**¼ cup honey**
**¾ cup frozen orange juice
   concentrate, thawed**

Combine water and honey until blended.
    Add juice concentrate and lemon juice and blend well.
    Serve over ice cubes and garnish with orange slices, if desired.

## • CAROB CLUSTERS •
10 minutes   2 dozen

½ cup noninstant dry milk
½ cup carob powder
½ cup hot water
2 tablespoons Butter's
  Brother (page 14)

1 cup peanuts
1 cup raisins

Combine the first 4 ingredients until thoroughly blended. Pour this mixture over peanuts and raisins and mix until well coated.

Drop mixture by teaspoonfuls onto a greased cookie sheet. Allow to air-dry for several hours.

Or put into a 300°F. oven until the tops are shiny and they can be removed from sheet, about 15 minutes. Chill.

Store in an airtight container in the refrigerator.

## • GORP •

Gorp is a mixture of dried fruits, nuts, and seeds. It is high in protein and full of quick energy. You can buy it commercially prepared in neat little plastic bags, but these are expensive. For a fraction of the cost, you can buy the ingredients and make it yourself. It can be made with practically anything in just about any amount. Use your imagination. Here is one typical recipe.

½ cup peanuts
½ cup sunflower seeds
½ cup chopped walnuts
¼ cup raisins

¼ cup chopped dried apricots
¼ cup raw or toasted sesame
  seeds

Toss and mix all ingredients until thoroughly blended.

Store in an airtight container. If you make large quantities, it will need to be refrigerated or kept in the freezer. Chances are it will disappear long before it spoils, however.

*Note:* Gorp can be quite high in calories as well as high in protein. If you want to lower the calorie content, reduce the amount of dried fruits and stick with nuts and seeds.

## • PEANUT-HONEY ROUNDS •
### 8 minutes    3 dozen

Kids love this recipe. They can help roll the mixture into rounds, then roll the rounds in carob and sesame seeds, and, best of all, eat the rounds.

| | |
|---|---|
| **2 cups peanuts** | **3 tablespoons raisins** |
| **5 tablespoons honey** | **2 tablespoons carob powder** |
| **1 tablespoon molasses** | **¼ cup sesame seeds** |

Blend the peanuts until they are finely ground.

Add honey, molasses, and raisins, and stir until well blended.

Roll mixture into small rounds or balls about 1 inch in diameter. Roll half of the balls in carob powder and the other half in sesame seeds. Set on wax paper.

Enjoy immediately or store in the refrigerator.

## • BANANA POM POMS •
### 7 minutes    Serves 4

| | |
|---|---|
| **1 teaspoon water** | **¼ cup finely chopped** |
| **1½ tablespoons carob powder** | **almonds, peanuts, or** |
| **2 teaspoons honey** | **walnuts** |
| **1 large banana** | |

Blend water and carob powder to make a paste. Stir in honey.

Cut banana into 8 pieces, about 1-inch lengths. Using a toothpick and spoon for easier handling, dip banana pieces into carob mixture, then into chopped nuts. Place on plastic-wrapped plate.

Freeze until firm. Wrap and store in freezer. Serve frozen.

## • FROZEN BANANA •
1 minute

A frozen banana is a wonderful summer snack. It's simple to make, as deliciously satisfying as ice cream, and can easily be dressed up enough to serve to company.

**For each serving:**

Peel a ripe, firm banana. Place it in a plastic bag, seal, and toss in the freezer. When it has frozen to the desired hardness, take it out and enjoy it. For easier handling, insert a wood popsicle stick into one end of the banana before it is frozen.

*Variations:*
Dip the banana in thawed orange juice concentrate. Roll in chopped coconut, peanuts, sesame seeds, or wheat germ; then freeze.
    Spread banana with peanut butter and freeze for two tastes in one. Garnish with peanuts, if desired.
    Dip banana in honey and roll in any of the above-mentioned garnishes; then freeze.
    Dip banana in Super Syrup (page 15), roll in chopped peanuts, and freeze.
    Dip banana in maple syrup and roll in shredded coconut, chopped nuts, or seeds. Freeze.

## • JUST JUICE CUBES •
5 minutes

Apple, cranberry, grape, and orange juice are excellent choices to use in this recipe. Or combine two or more juices for even more flavor.
    Pour juice of your choice into plastic popsicle molds, ice cube trays, or paper cups. Insert wood popsicle sticks or toothpicks into mixture in ice cube trays or paper cups just as it begins to harden

but is still mushy. Place in the freezer and allow to harden before serving.


## • PUDDING-ON-A-STICK •

Follow the recipes for:

| | |
|---|---|
| Almost Chocolate Pudding | (page 56) |
| No-Cook "Banilla" Pudding | (page 55) |
| Presto Pumpkin Pudding | (page 34) |

Instead of plopping pudding into bowls, spoon pudding into pop-sicle molds or paper cups. Insert wood sticks to use as handles and stick them in the freezer. Be as patient as possible in waiting for them to harden.


## • YOGURT-FRUIT DELIGHT •
### 6 minutes   Serves 4

This is a good basic recipe with many variations. Try whatever fruit, nut, or seed combination catches your fancy.

**2 cups plain yogurt**

Put yogurt in a bowl and place in the freezer until it is mushy. Remove from freezer and beat thoroughly.
  Add one of the following fruit suggestions and beat again:

| | |
|---|---|
| **2 cups slightly mashed blueberries, raspberries, or strawberries** | **1½ cups pitted, chunked cherries** |
| **2 bananas, chunked** | **2 cups chunked peaches** |
| | **2 cups crushed pineapple** |

Return mixture to the freezer again and allow to harden.
  You can also add honey to taste if this recipe is too tart for your kids.

## • YOGURT POPS •
5 minutes    Serves 6

A great summer snack.

**1 6-ounce can frozen orange
    juice concentrate, thawed**

**2 cups plain yogurt
2 teaspoons vanilla extract**

Combine all the ingredients and blend until smooth. Pour mixture into paper cups and insert wood sticks, or pour into popsicle molds. Freeze until firm.

## • PEANUT BUTTER AND . . . •
5 minutes

A peanut butter and jelly sandwich is an old standby and a great one too. But have you ever thought of:

peanut butter and . . .
    grated carrots and raisins
    cottage cheese, apple slices, and raisins
    cream cheese with crushed pineapple
    honey on whole wheat toast or a
       toasted English muffin
    honey with crushed or sliced fruit
       (apples, dates, and oranges are good)
    jelly and banana slices
    jelly and cream cheese
    mayonnaise
    coconut, chopped nuts, sesame seeds,
       sprouts and/or sunflower seeds

## • MILD TUNA MEDLEY •
### 5 minutes   Serves 4-6

Just stir and you have a protein-rich sandwich filling, a dip to serve with vegetables, or a salad on a bed of lettuce.

**1 cup cottage cheese**
**1 6-ounce can water-packed tuna, well drained**

Blend cheese and tuna thoroughly. Refrigerate until ready to use. Just before serving, stir in one of the following ingredients:

| | |
|---|---|
| avocado slices | pickle relish |
| chopped celery | sprouts |
| grated cheese | sunflower seeds |
| cucumber slices | diced tomatoes |
| sliced hard-boiled eggs | wheat germ |
| diced green pepper | |

## • BRITISH BANANA SANDWICH •
### 2 minutes

**For each serving:**

**1-2 tablespoons peanut butter**
**2 slices whole wheat bread,**
  **toasted**

**2 tablespoons sesame seeds**
**1 banana, sliced**

Spread peanut butter on 1 slice of toast. Sprinkle with sesame seeds and top with banana slices. Place the other slice of toast on top and serve.

*Variation:*
  Serve as an open-faced sandwich and warm slightly under the broiler before adding banana slices.

## • RICOTTA/CREAM CHEESE SANDWICHES •
### 5 minutes

Cheese is a protein-packed food and most kids like its creamy, smooth consistency. If you haven't thought of serving this type of sandwich before, read on and try some of our suggestions the next time you hear "I'm hungry, what have we got to eat?"

Ricotta or cream cheese plain on whole wheat toast or on any fruit or nut quick bread is great-tasting. Some excellent variations include:

| | |
|---|---|
| cinnamon | chopped nuts |
| crushed or sliced fruit | Parmesan cheese |
| gorp | peanut butter |
| granola | seeds |
| honey | strawberries |
| fruit jams or jelly | wheat germ |

For even more variety, try broiling any of these combinations.

# · Quick and Easy ·

When you are in a real pinch for time, 15 minutes can seem like forever. You have umpteen other things to do and the kids are hungry, but you still want to supply a nutritious treat. For times like these, all the recipes in this Quick and Easy section can be made and ready to serve in 5 minutes tops.

We have not included any drinks under Quick and Easy, so please flip through the chapter on Drinks and consider them the next time you need a fast snack. You will be pleasantly surprised at how varied, filling, and quick they are.

## · APPLE WHIP ·
### 5 minutes    Serves 4

**1 cup applesauce**                        **1 tablespoon honey**
**2 egg whites**

Blend all the ingredients until the mixture is thick, white, and creamy. Spoon into glasses and serve immediately.

45

## • BROILED CINNAMON APPLES •
5 minutes   Serves 2

1 apple
1 teaspoon butter or Butter's
  Brother (page 14)

1 teaspoon cinnamon
1 teaspoon (scant) honey

Cut the apple in half. Scoop out the center and fill each hole with ½ teaspoon of butter.

Mix the cinnamon and honey and sprinkle on the cut surfaces of apple.

Place apples, cut side up, in a baking pan. Broil 5-7 inches from heat for about 5 minutes, or until butter melts and bubbles. Serve immediately.

## • BANANA BOATS •
5 minutes   Serves 2

1 teaspoon orange juice
1 teaspoon honey

1 ripe banana

Mix orange juice and honey until blended.

Cut off each end of the banana. Leave the peel on and cut banana in half lengthwise. Place halves, cut side up, on a broiling pan. Brush each half with honey/juice mixture.

Broil 5-7 inches from heat for 3-5 minutes, or until banana is soft, bubbly, and brown. Serve immediately. Scoop banana from its boat with a spoon.

## • FRIED BANANAS •
5 minutes    Serves 2

**1½ teaspoons vegetable oil**
**2 bananas, peeled and cut into**
  **¼-½-inch slices**

**Shredded coconut or finely**
  **chopped nuts (optional)**

Place oil in a skillet. Add banana slices and fry until they are golden brown. Turn once and cook on the other side. Remove from pan and garnish with coconut or nuts.
  Serve immediately.

## • BOUILLON •
3 minutes

Be sure to buy unsalted bouillon, which is available in health food stores and most grocery stores.
  It takes only a minute or two to pour boiling water into a cup or bowl, add a bouillon cube, stir well, and you have a hot, nourishing snack. Serve immediately.

*Variations:*
  Add leftover rice, noodles, pasta, or chopped vegetables.
  Sprinkle with grated cheese.
  Drop in a raw egg and stir well.
  Add croutons, sprinkle with mozzarella cheese, and broil until cheese melts.

## CHEESE, FRUIT, AND VEGETABLE COMBINATIONS
### 5 minutes

Many of the following snack ideas are ones you have probably already thought of, and they may now be old standbys in your snack repertoire.

Although these are not specific recipes, the combinations are useful because at least two or three of these foods are sure to be in your refrigerator at all times, so you can always rely on them when you are in a pinch for time and inspiration.

We have listed a number of combinations in an effort to give you some new ways of serving these familiar foods in an attractive and fast fashion. We hope we have hit upon some that you might not have thought of.

*Hard and semi-hard cheeses* (like Cheddar, Monterey Jack, mozzarella, and Muenster) may be cut into cubes and speared on toothpicks alternately with chunks of fruit and vegetables.

*Soft cheeses* (like cottage, cream and ricotta cheeses) *plus sour cream and plain yogurt* may be mixed with chunked, grated, or sliced fruit or vegetables, and simply served in a bowl as a snack or a dip. Or they can be served as a spread on crackers, bread, and other fruits and vegetables.

You can serve many combinations in paper cups for easier handling; it's just the right amount for children, too.

Added garnishes of shredded coconut, gorp, granola, nuts, seeds, and sprouts will enhance the flavor and nutritional value of these combinations.

Be sure to store these foods in covered containers in the refrigerator or freezer.

### FRUITS
apple/banana/yogurt/nuts
apple/blue cheese
apple/Cheddar cheese
apple/pineapple/cottage cheese

apple/peanut butter
applesauce/cottage cheese
banana/dates/orange chunks
banana/orange chunks/strawberries
banana/peach/pineapple/strawberries
banana/pear/Muenster cheese
banana/strawberries/nuts/yogurt
blueberries/grapefruit/orange chunks
green grapes/Swiss cheese
melon/blueberries/grapes/orange chunks
melon/raspberries/almonds
orange chunks/celery/nuts
orange chunks/cream cheese
peaches/banana/coconut
peaches/pineapple/celery/nuts
peaches/raspberries/cottage cheese
pears/Cheddar cheese
pears/Muenster cheese
pineapple/cream or cottage cheese/nuts

## VEGETABLES

carrots/peanut butter
carrots/cream cheese/nuts
carrots/cottage cheese or plain yogurt/orange chunks
celery/peanut butter
celery/cottage cheese
celery/grated Parmesan cheese
celery/cream cheese
celery/tuna salad
celery/egg salad
cucumber/sour cream/minced onions
lettuce or spinach/cream cheese, mayonnaise, egg salad,
    or tuna salad rolled up inside
pickles/cottage cheese/minced garlic
radishes, split and filled/cottage cheese
tomatoes/cottage cheese/sunflower seeds
tomatoes/tuna salad
zucchini/sliced hard-boiled eggs

## • O.G.'S BONNET EGGS •
### 4 minutes

Sometimes all that is needed is a little imagination to change the humdrum into a flight of fancy for a child. Jan's grandmother gave this old standby a new name and made eating eggs a lot more fun.

Bonnet eggs are simply semi-hard-boiled eggs (cook about 10 minutes). Peel off the shell, stand egg on end, and slice in half. The sunny yellow yolk is the "face" surrounded by the white bonnet.

Serve on bread or toast, if desired.

## • NANNY'S GREAT GRAPE COMPOTE •
### 5 minutes   Serves 2-3

Melinda found this recipe in an antique recipe box that belonged to her grandmother. It can easily be doubled to serve a larger number of kids.

1 tablespoon honey
½ tablespoon lemon juice
1½ cups green seedless
  grapes

¾ cup cottage or ricotta
  cheese
Cinnamon

Mix the honey and lemon juice. Toss with grapes.

Beat cheese until it is smooth. Spoon over grapes. Sprinkle on cinnamon.

Serve at once or store in a covered container in refrigerator.

*Variations:*
Sprinkle coconut, gorp, granola, nuts, or seeds over grapes.
Experiment with other fruits your children like.
Try freezing honeyed grapes for a different snack. Serve them partially thawed with cheese and cinnamon.

## • GOLDEN GRAPEFRUIT •
5 minutes   Serves 2

**1 grapefruit**                                    **½ cup honey**

Cut grapefruit in half. Cut meat from skin completely around fruit; then cut meat into sections. Drizzle honey over both halves. Broil grapefruit halves until honey is bubbly and grapefruit is heated through. Serve immediately.

*Variations:*
    After removing grapefruit from broiler, sprinkle with shredded coconut, granola, gorp, wheat germ, or chopped nuts.
    Mix ¼ cup of honey with ¼ cup of molasses to drizzle on grapefruit.

## • INSTANT ITALIAN ICE •
4 minutes   Serves 4

Children love this super-fast fruit slush.

**¾ cup frozen orange juice**                       **2 cups ice cubes**
**concentrate**

Blend frozen juice concentrate and ice cubes (add one at a time) in a blender or food processor until mixture is smooth, about 2 minutes. Serve immediately or store in the freezer.

*Variations*
    Experiment with other fruit juice concentrate flavors, such as apple, grape, or grapefruit.

## • NUT BUTTER •
5 minutes   2 cups

Peanut butter is the most well-known nut butter (see Real Peanut Butter, page 16). But other kinds of nuts and seeds are just as versatile and delicious ground into butters.

2 cups almonds, pecans,                    ¼ cup vegetable oil
   pumpkin seeds, sesame
   seeds, sunflower seeds, or
   walnuts

Blend nuts or seeds in a blender or food processor until finely ground, about 1 minute. Gradually add the oil, a tablespoon at a time, while continuing to blend until the mixture is smooth.
   Store in an airtight container and refrigerate.


*Variation:*
   Mix nut butter with cottage cheese, cream cheese, or ricotta cheese to make a deliciously different spread or dip.


## • PINEAPPLE SHERBET •
3 minutes   Serves 4

The secret of this surprisingly easy and undeniably delicious goodie is to always keep a can (20-ounce size is good) of unsweetened pineapple chunks in the freezer. When the urge for something creamy, cool, and rich strikes, you can literally whip up this recipe.
   Blend slightly thawed pineapple chunks in a blender or food processor until they are smooth, thick, and creamy, about 2 minutes. Serve immediately.

### • POPCORN •
5 minutes   4 quarts

Popcorn is a favorite snack for all ages. Not only is it fun to make, good-tasting, and nutritious, it is even beneficial to healthy teeth.

It is not good for you, however, dripping with butter or loaded with salt. Allow its own natural flavor to come through by omitting both of these.

Buy popping corn in bulk from a co-op, if possible. It's cheaper that way and the kernels can be frozen and stored for about 12 months.

**2 tablespoons vegetable oil**                    **1 cup popping corn**

Pour oil into a large pan. Add corn and cover with a tight-fitting lid. Cook over medium heat, shaking pan gently to prevent popcorn from burning. When popping stops, remove pan from heat and pour popped popcorn into a large bowl.

Store in an airtight container.

*Variations:*

Popcorn can also be used to decorate your home. String it (with cranberries, if you like) to create garlands for your Christmas tree. It can be pressed into balls for a sure-fire Halloween treat and even spiced-up for an entirely new taste sensation (see Spicy Popcorn, page 54, Warm Cheese Popcorn, page 54, or Curry Corn, page 143).

If you ever get to the point where you just can't stand the thought of another bite of popcorn (hard to believe, we know), pop up a batch for our feathered friends. They are as crazy about it as we are.

## • SPICY POPCORN •
5 minutes  2 quarts

**2 quarts, popped popcorn
(about ½ cup pre-popped)**
**¼ cup butter or Butter's
Brother (page 14)**

**½ teaspoon cinnamon**
**¼ teaspoon nutmeg**

Put popcorn in a large bowl.

Melt butter in saucepan. Stir cinnamon and nutmeg into melted butter.

Pour mixture over popcorn and toss until well coated.

Store in an airtight container.

## • WARM CHEESE POPCORN •
5 minutes  1 quart

**1-1½ tablespoons vegetable
oil**
**1½ teaspoons Parmesan
cheese**

**¾ teaspoon each chives, dill
seed and celery seed or
garlic powder**
**4 cups popped popcorn**

Heat oil in a large skillet or saucepan.

Add remaining ingredients and stir until popcorn is warm and well coated.

Pour popcorn into a bowl to serve.

Store in an airtight container.

## • MASHED POTATO SOUP •
### 5 minutes

A great way to use those leftover mashed potatoes is to mix them with milk over low heat. Add just enough milk so that potatoes have a souplike consistency but are still creamy and thick. Stir constantly to ensure smoothness. Season to taste. Top with grated cheese and serve immediately.

## • NO-COOK "BANILLA" PUDDING •
### 5 minutes   Serves 4

This quick and easy pudding is made in a blender or food processor with hard-boiled eggs.

½ cup water
½ cup vegetable oil
¼ cup honey
1 tablespoon vanilla extract

1 banana, peeled and
  chunked
3 shelled, hard-boiled eggs

Blend the first 4 ingredients until mixture is smooth. Add the banana and eggs as you continue blending until smooth again. Chill pudding before serving.

Store in the refrigerator or freeze.

## • ALMOST CHOCOLATE PUDDING •
5 minutes   Serves 4

A simply scrumptious pudding that your children will love. It's so close to chocolate pudding in looks and taste that you might feel guilty serving it.

½ cup water
½ cup vegetable oil
¼ cup honey

1 teaspoon vanilla extract
½ cup carob powder
3 shelled, hard-boiled eggs

Blend the first 4 ingredients until mixture is smooth. Add carob powder and eggs and continue blending until smooth again. Chill pudding before serving.

Store in the refrigerator or freeze.

## • RICE CREAM •
5 minutes   Serves 4

2 cups heavy cream
1 teaspoon vanilla extract

⅓ cup honey
1 cup cooked brown rice

Whip cream and vanilla. Just as it begins to thicken, drizzle in honey. Add rice and beat again. Spoon mixture into individual dishes and chill thoroughly before serving.

Store in an airtight container and refrigerate.

## SANDWICH FILLINGS

Many sandwich fillings are quick and easy snack ideas. They can be served as sandwiches on bread or crackers, stuffed into such vegetables as carrots, celery, green peppers, and tomatoes, or rolled up in lettuce or spinach leaves.

*Cheese*—plain or broiled
        sliced vegetables such as tomatoes, onions, or lettuce

*Chicken (Sliced) or Chicken Salad*—plain or broiled/with cheese/tomato and lettuce/hard-boiled egg and lettuce/tomato and grated cheese/apple chunks, celery, and walnuts

*Cream Cheese*—on date-nut bread/other nut breads/with strawberries/pineapple chunks/orange chunks/fruit butters/sour cream and chopped cucumber/chopped chicken

*Egg Salad*—with diced carrots/chopped celery and onions/chopped pickle/grated cheese

*Peanut Butter*—with jelly/sliced bananas/crushed pineapple/chopped pickle/mayonnaise/raisins/coconut/sprouts/grated carrot

*Tomato*—on bread with butter

*Tuna Salad*—chopped vegetables/cheese/pickles

# · Drinks ·

Our drinks just might be the easiest and fastest way to get those much needed nutrients into your kids.

Nothing satisfies like a tall, cool drink on a hot day, and a drink can also be a substantial meal-in-itself eye-opener to get everyone off in the morning. Whether it be a before-bedtime snack, a mid-morning break, or a party refreshment, we have an assortment of drinks to please everyone. You'll be pleased at how quickly these drinks can be whipped up too.

## Some Tips

Fresh fruit can always be substituted for any canned or frozen varieties called for in the recipes.

For a frothy milkshake consistency, add ice cubes, one at a time, while the drink is being processed in a blender or food processor at high speed.

To solve the problem of a lukewarm drink in a lunch box, *partially* fill a thermos with the beverage the night before and freeze. In the morning, fill the thermos completely. By lunchtime the frozen beverage will have thawed and the drink will still be icy cold.

When buying lemon juice, be sure it contains no additives. The frozen variety may be the best choice.

### • APPLE SNOW •
5 minutes    Serves 2

**6-7 tablespoons frozen apple
  juice concentrate,
  partially thawed**

**½ cup water
8 ice cubes**

Blend juice concentrate and water in a blender or food processor. Increase speed to high and drop in ice cubes, one at a time. Whirl until thickened. Serve immediately.

### • CREAMY APRICOT FIZZ •
5 minutes    Serves 2

You can make this recipe—minus the sparkling water—ahead of time and refrigerate it for several hours. Add sparkling water just before serving.

**2 cups canned apricot halves,
  drained
1 cup plain yogurt
2 eggs**

**⅓ cup noninstant dry milk
½ cup natural sparkling water**

Blend the first 4 ingredients until smooth. Pour mixture into glasses and add sparkling water. Stir and serve immediately.

## • BLUEBERRY BLEND •
5 minutes    Serves 2

1 cup fresh or frozen
 blueberries

2 cups milk
1 teaspoon honey

Blend ingredients until blueberries are completely broken up and milk is purple and frothy. Serve immediately.

*Variation:*
 Substitute 2 cups fresh or frozen strawberries for blueberries and add 2 teaspoons of vanilla extract. Blend.

## • CAROBANANA •
5 minutes    Serves 2

2 cups milk
1 banana
1 egg

¼ cup honey
1 tablespoon carob powder

Blend the first 4 ingredients together. Add carob powder and continue blending until mixture is smooth. Serve immediately.

*Variations:*
 YOGURT YUMMY—Simply substitute 1 cup of plain yogurt for the 1 cup of milk. The result is smooth and tangy.
 Try adding ¼ cup of strawberries and ¼ cup of apple or pineapple juice to either recipe.
 Blend in 2 or 3 ice cubes, one at a time, for a thicker texture.

## • CRAN-APPLE DRINK •
2 minutes   Serves 2

1 cup orange juice
¼ cup cranberries
1 tablespoon honey

1 medium-size apple, chunked

Blend all ingredients in a blender or food processor until fruit is finely chopped and mixture is smooth. Serve immediately.

## • CUCUMBER COOLER •
5 minutes   Serves 2

Most cucumbers found in grocery stores have been coated with a layer of wax to preserve them. Although this wax is supposed to be edible, we recommend you peel the cucumbers in all our recipes.

1-1½ cucumbers, peeled and chunked
1 cup plain yogurt

2 tablespoons mint leaves, preferably fresh
3 ice cubes

Put the first 3 ingredients into a blender or food processor and blend until smooth.

Continue blending at high speed and add ice cubes, one at a time, until drink is thick and ice is finely chopped. Serve immediately.

# • EGGNOG •
5 minutes    Serves 2

**2 cups cold milk**
**2 eggs**
**1½ tablespoons honey**

**½ teaspoon vanilla extract**
**Nutmeg**

Blend the first 4 ingredients until mixture is creamy and smooth. Pour into glasses, sprinkle with nutmeg, and serve.

*Variations:*
   Add a mashed banana or fruit of your choice and blend in well.
   Pour eggnog into paper cups or plastic popsicle molds and freeze.
   Partially thawed frozen eggnog is very good served over fresh fruit or cake.

# • FLORIDA FANTASTIC •
2 minutes    Serves 2

Jan's Aunt Anne invented this cooling breakfast treat. She lives in Florida and makes it with fresh orange juice.

**1 frozen banana**                    **2 cups orange juice**

Put ingredients in a blender or food processor and blend until mixture is smooth. Serve immediately.

## • FRUIT COOLER •
### 5 minutes    Serves 2

½ cups cold water
2 heaping tablespoons *each,* partially thawed: frozen apple
   juice concentrate, frozen orange juice concentrate, and frozen
   pineapple juice concentrate

Blend all ingredients until mixture is smooth. Serve immediately.

## • FRUTTI FIZZ •
### 5 minutes    Serves 2

1 cup apple or orange juice          ¼ cup nuts
½ cup strawberries, chunked          ⅔ cup melon, chunked

Blend all ingredients until mixture is smooth. Serve immediately.

## • JIM'S INSTANT BREAKFAST •
### 5 minutes    Serves 2

Jan's dad, Jim Wilder, says that blending this drink at two speeds
prevents the wheat germ from settling at the bottom of the glass.

1 frozen banana, chunked          1 teaspoon vanilla extract
4 eggs                            2-3 cups milk
4 tablespoons wheat germ

Place the first 4 ingredients in a blender or food processor. Pour
in milk until it reaches the "3 cup" mark. Blend at low speed for
1 minute, or until the banana is broken up. Increase speed to

high and continue blending 2 more minutes. Pour mixture into glasses and serve immediately.

## • LIQUID GOLD •
### 3 minutes   Serves 4

Liquid Gold can sit in your refrigerator a day or two.

**1 6-ounce can frozen orange
    juice concentrate, thawed
1 cup milk
1 cup water**

**¼ cup honey
1 teaspoon vanilla extract
10-12 ice cubes**

Combine the first 5 ingredients in a blender or food processor at high speed.

Add ice cubes, one at a time, and continue blending until cubes are finely chopped and drink is thick and creamy. Serve immediately or store in the refrigerator.

*Variation:*

LIQUID GOLD CREAMSICLES—Pour mixture into paper cups or plastic popsicle molds and freeze.

## • FANCY DANCY LEMONADE •
### 10 minutes   Serves 4

**4 cups water
½ cup lemon juice
½ orange, chunked**

**¼ cup pineapple juice
½ cup honey**

Heat water to boiling.

Combine lemon, orange, and pineapple juices until well mixed.

Add fruit juice mixture and honey to the boiling water and stir.

Chill and stir before serving over ice. Store in the refrigerator.

## • MILKSHAKE •
5 minutes    Serves 2

Milkshakes are everybody's favorite drink. Depending on the ingredients you use, they can be a nutritious snack, a drink with meals, or even breakfast.

In a blender or food processor, blend 2 cups of milk with one or more of the following combinations and serve warm or cold:

**4 tablespoons peanut butter with honey to taste**

**2 teaspoons honey with pinch of cinnamon or nutmeg**

**4 tablespoons molasses**

**¾ cup fresh fruit with honey to taste**

**1 mashed banana with honey to taste**

**2 carrots, chunked into small pieces**

**2 or 3 tablespoons Super Syrup (p. 15) for a chocolate shake**

*Variations:*

For added nutrition, include bran, wheat germ, or an egg in any shake.

For a thicker, creamier shake, add ice cubes, one at a time, while drink is being blended at high speed.

## · HOT MULLED PINE/APPLE JUICE ·
5 minutes    Serves 6

**1 46-ounce can unsweetened**
**pineapple or apple juice**

**2 cinnamon sticks**
**6 whole cloves**

Combine ingredients in a saucepan and bring to a boil over medium heat. Reduce heat, cover pan, and simmer mixture for 10 minutes.

Remove from heat and discard the cinnamon sticks and cloves.

Serve immediately or store in a covered container in the refrigerator. Reheat before serving.

*Variations:*

Substitute apple cider for apple or pineapple juice to make MARVELOUS MULLED CIDER.

Add a few cranberries for color, tang, and spice.

## · PEACHY CREAMY ·
5 minutes    Serves 2

**1 cup canned peaches,**
**drained**
**2 cups milk**

**¼ teaspoon ground ginger**
**1 tablespoon honey**

Blend the first 3 ingredients in a blender or food processor until the mixture is smooth.

Add honey and blend until frothy. Serve immediately.

## • THICK AND LUSCIOUS BANANA CREAM •
### 5 minutes   Serves 2

The secret of this creamy, incredibly thick drink is the crushed ice. Whole ice cubes, added one at a time, work just as well, however.

**1 banana, chunked**                    **¼ teaspoon vanilla extract**
**½ cup milk**                            **1 cup crushed ice**
**1 tablespoon honey**

Combine all the ingredients in a blender or food processor and blend until mixture is smooth. Serve immediately.

*Variation:*
  Substitute a frozen banana and omit the crushed ice.

## • WATERMELON WHOOPEE •
### 5 minutes   Serves 2

**2 cups watermelon, chunked**           **1 tablespoon honey**
**2 tablespoons lemon juice**

Liquefy watermelon chunks in a blender or food processor. Add lemon juice and honey and blend. Serve over ice.

# · Breads and Muffins ·

Not many children can resist a moist slice of mellow banana bread . . . warm blueberry muffins chock full of plump berries . . . or golden cornbread so tender it crumbles in their hands and melts in their mouths.

These are just a few of the baked goods we call "quick" because the leavening agents that are used—baking powder, baking soda, and air—make them rise so quickly they are ready to be baked as soon as they are mixed.

We've taken many old favorites, and some soon-to-be new ones we're sure, and made them more healthful, nutritious, and delicious. You won't have to worry when these snacks disappear quickly.

## Some Tips

The secret to making light quick breads and muffins is to never overmix the batter. Stir just until it is moistened.

To make light airy muffins, mix the wet and dry ingredients thoroughly but separately. Then blend them together quickly until the batter is smooth.

Muffin batters made with whole wheat flour tend to be heavy and require a little different handling. For a nice, high, rounded muffin, fill the muffin cups to the top with batter and bake as directed in the recipe.

You will notice the phrase "test for doneness" at the end of many of the bread and muffin recipes. The method we use to test doneness is to insert a toothpick into the center; if it comes out clean and dry, the bread and/or muffins are done. If batter or soft crumbs remain on the toothpick, bake a few minutes longer and retest.

For easy unmolding of muffins, try greasing not only the inside of the muffin cup but also the top of the tins. After baking, run a thin, sharp knife around the rim of the cup and gently lift the muffin out.

To reheat quick breads or muffins, wrap them in aluminum foil and place them in a warm (250°F.) oven for 10-15 minutes. Muffins can also be split and placed on a cookie sheet to be reheated in a warm oven or split and popped right into a toaster.

Baked goods can be stored either at room temperature or in the refrigerator as long as they are properly and tightly wrapped in aluminum foil, plastic wrap, or placed in an airtight container.

## Freezing Breads and Muffins

We recommend baking breads and muffins before freezing. Unbaked products may become tough and have a poor texture.

Before freezing quick bread, slice it in half or into quarters. Wrap each section separately and then place in the freezer. This keeps the bread fresher and allows you to thaw just the amount you need. It also decreases the amount of time it takes to freeze and thaw. Be sure to mark clearly what it is.

Most quick breads and muffins can be kept frozen between 2 and 3 months.

To thaw, allow bread or muffins to stand at room temperature or warm them in a 325°F. oven. Muffins can be split and popped in the toaster for faster thawing.

## • APPLE BREAD •
12 minutes   2 loaves

Rich, moist, and sweet with the delightful combination of fresh apple and crunchy nuts.

2 eggs
¾ cup honey
½ cup vegetable oil
¼ cup plain yogurt
1 teaspoon vanilla extract

1 teaspoon baking soda
2½ cups unbleached flour
¾ cup chopped walnuts
1 medium apple, chunked

Preheat oven 350°F.
   Blend the first 5 ingredients. Add baking soda and mix. Stir in flour. Fold in walnuts and then apples.
   Pour batter into 2 well-greased 9 x 5 x 3-inch loaf pans.
   Bake 45 minutes. Test for doneness. Remove to wire racks to cool.

## • BANANA-NUT BREAD •
12 minutes   2 loaves

2½ cups unbleached flour
¾ cup honey
3½ teaspoons baking powder
3 tablespoons vegetable oil
¾ cup milk

1 egg
1 cup mashed banana (about
   2-3 medium-sized ones)
1 cup chopped nuts

Preheat oven 350°F.
   Measure all the ingredients into a large bowl and beat until thoroughly mixed.
   Pour batter into 2 well-greased 9 x 5 x 3-inch loaf pans.
   Bake 55-65 minutes. Test for doneness. Remove bread from pans. Cool before slicing.

## • BEST BLUEBERRY MUFFINS •
8 minutes    1 dozen

2 cups unbleached flour
1 tablespoon baking powder
½ teaspoon cinnamon
1½-2 cups fresh or frozen
    blueberries

½ cup vegetable oil
⅓ cup honey
½ cup milk
2 eggs
½ teaspoon vanilla extract

Preheat oven 425°F.
   In a large bowl, whisk the first 3 ingredients.
   Sprinkle berries with 1 tablespoon of the dry ingredients; toss and set aside.
   Beat oil, honey, milk, eggs, and vanilla until mixture is smoothly blended. Add this mixture to the dry ingredients and blend until moistened. Fold in berries. Spoon batter into greased muffin tins.
   Bake 15 minutes. Allow to cool before removing from tins.

## • BANANA-ORANGE BREAD •
10 minutes    2 large loaves

Marmalade and coconut give this old favorite a new twist.

½ cup vegetable oil
⅔ cup honey
3 bananas, chunked
¼ cup orange marmalade
2 eggs
1 cup unbleached flour

½ cup whole wheat flour
½ cup bran
1 teaspoon baking soda
¼ cup chopped walnuts or
    pecans
¼ cup shredded unsweetened
    coconut

Preheat oven 375°F.
   Combine oil and honey. Beat in bananas, marmalade, and eggs.

Whisk flours, bran, and baking soda. Add to banana mixture and mix well. Stir in nuts and coconut.

Pour batter into 2 well-greased 9 x 5 x 3-inch loaf pans.

Bake 40-45 minutes. Test for doneness.

*Variation:*

INDIVIDUAL BANANA-ORANGE BREADS—Divide the batter of Banana-Orange Bread between 5 clean, well-greased soup cans (10¾-ounce size). Bake the same amount of time as for larger loaves.

Individual snack breads are just the right size for break time. They can be popped out of the freezer and thawed much more quickly than the loaf size.

## • BRAISIN-RAISIN MUFFINS •
6 minutes    1½ dozen

1½ cups bran
1 cup whole wheat flour
½ cup raisins
1 teaspoon baking soda
1 teaspoon cinnamon
1 teaspoon nutmeg
1 egg

¼ cup chopped nuts (almonds and walnuts are good choices)
2 tablespoons vegetable oil
½ cup honey
1 teaspoon vanilla extract
¾ cup milk

Preheat oven 375°F.

In a large bowl, whisk the first 6 ingredients and make a well. Add the remaining ingredients and stir until mixture is blended.

Add 1 heaping tablespoon of batter to each greased muffin cup.

Bake 12-15 minutes, or until muffins are puffy and firm.

## • BROWN BREAD •
8 minutes   1 loaf

Munchy, crunchy bread sweet with the rich taste of molasses. Especially good served with cottage or cream cheese and topped with sliced fruit.

**2 cups whole wheat flour**
**½ cup wheat germ or bran**
**1 teaspoon baking soda**

**½ cup molasses**
**1½ cups plain yogurt**
**½ cup raisins**

Preheat oven 350°F.
    In a large bowl, combine the first 3 ingredients.
    Mix molasses and yogurt. Add to the dry ingredients and blend well. Stir in raisins.
    Pour batter into greased loaf pan.
    Bake 45-50 minutes. Test for doneness.

## • BUSY BAKEQUICK BISCUITS •
7 minutes   1-1½ dozen

**2 cups Busy Bakequick (page 20)**
**¼ cup vegetable oil**

**¾ cup milk**

Preheat oven to 450°F.
    Mix all ingredients thoroughly.
    Roll dough out between wax paper to ½-inch thickness. Cut out with a floured cutter or the edge of a glass, and place rounds on a greased cookie sheet.
    Bake 10-12 minutes.

## • BUSY BAKEQUICK MUFFINS •
### 5 minutes   1 dozen

2 cups Busy Bakequick (page
    20)
½ cup vegetable oil

1 egg
¼ cup honey
¾ cup milk

Preheat oven to 400°F.
Mix ingredients until they are thoroughly blended but the batter is still lumpy. Spoon batter into greased muffin tins until two-thirds full.
Bake 25 minutes.

## • BAKED CHEESE RING •
### 8 minutes   1 large cake (Serves 8-10)

2 cups unbleached flour
3 teaspoons baking powder
1 cup grated Cheddar cheese,
    divided

1 egg
¼ cup vegetable oil
1 cup milk

Preheat oven to 400°F.
In a large bowl, whisk flour to lighten. Add baking powder and whisk again. Stir in ¾ cup grated cheese.
Combine the remaining ingredients and add to the flour mixture. Stir with a fork just until the batter is moist but still lumpy. Pour batter into a greased 8-inch bundt pan. Sprinkle with remaining cheese.
Bake 20-25 minutes. Test for doneness.

## • QUICK CHEESE BREAD •
### 10 minutes    1 loaf

This bread is so good warm that it's worth the extra few minutes it takes to heat it each time you serve it.

**2 eggs**
**1¼ cups milk**
**3 cups Busy Bakequick (page 20)**

**2 cups shredded Cheddar cheese**

Preheat oven to 350°F.

Blend eggs and milk. Add Busy Bakequick and stir until batter is moistened. Stir in shredded cheese. Pour mixture into a greased 9 x 5 x 3-inch loaf pan.

Bake 45 minutes. Crust will be crisp, so test for doneness in the center of loaf. Remove from pan and enjoy while still warm.

## • SURPRISE CHEESE MUFFINS •
### 7 minutes    1 dozen

Everyone loves to be surprised.

**1 egg**
**¼ cup vegetable oil**
**1 cup milk**
**2 cups unbleached flour**

**3 teaspoons baking powder**
**Cheddar or Swiss cheese cut into 1-inch cubes**

Preheat oven to 400°F.

Beat the egg. Add oil and milk and blend.

Whisk flour and baking powder. Add to wet mixture and stir until batter is just moist and still lumpy. Do not overmix.

Fill greased muffin tins two-thirds full. Press 1 cheese cube into the center of each muffin. Cover with remaining batter.
Bake 20-25 minutes. Remove from the pan immediately.

## • CRANBERRY BREAD •
10 minutes   2 loaves or 3 dozen muffins

This is one bread that slices better the next day.

**4 cups unbleached flour**
**1 tablespoon baking powder**
**1 teaspoon baking soda**
**½ teaspoon cinnamon**
**¼ teaspoon nutmeg**
**½ cup vegetable oil**
**1½ cups honey**

**1 tablespoon grated orange peel**
**1½ cups orange juice**
**2 eggs**
**2 cups whole cranberries**
**1 cup chopped nuts**
**⅔ cup raisins**

Preheat oven to 350°F.
Whisk the first 5 ingredients in a large bowl.
Combine the oil, honey, orange peel, juice, and eggs. Add to the dry ingredients and mix until batter is just moistened. Fold in the remaining ingredients. Pour batter into 2 greased 9 x 5 x 3-inch loaf pans.
Bake 55-65 minutes. Test for doneness and allow to cool.

*Variation:*
Substitute ¾ cup of lemon juice and ¾ cup of water for the orange juice.

## • CRUNCHY CRANBERRY MUFFINS •
6 minutes    1 dozen

1½ cups unbleached flour
1 cup rolled oats
1 tablespoon baking powder
1 teaspoon cinnamon
1 cup fresh or frozen
   cranberries

¼ cup vegetable oil
⅓ cup honey
1 cup milk
1 egg

Preheat oven to 425°F.
   In a large bowl, whisk the first 4 ingredients. Save 1 tablespoon of this mixture and toss with the cranberries; set aside.
   Blend the oil, honey, milk, and egg. Add to dry ingredients and mix. Fold in cranberries. Spoon batter into greased muffin cups.
   Bake 15-20 minutes. Cool 5 minutes before removing muffins from tins.

## • DATE-NUT BREAD •
10 minutes    2 loaves

2½ cups unbleached flour
3 tablespoons vegetable oil
¾ cup honey
3½ teaspoons baking powder

1¼ cups milk
1 egg
1 cup chopped dates
1 cup chopped nuts

Preheat oven to 350°F.
   Combine all ingredients and blend until mixture is smooth.
   Pour into 2 greased 9 x 5 x 3-inch loaf pans.
   Bake 55-65 minutes. Test for doneness. Remove from pan and let bread cool before slicing.
   Serve with cream cheese (plain or with pineapple), cottage cheese, or ricotta.

## • FRAGRANT HERB BREAD •
7 minutes     1 loaf

1½ cups unbleached flour
1½ cups whole wheat flour
2 teaspoons baking powder
2 teaspoons baking soda
1 cup plain yogurt
1 tablespoon parsley
1 tablespoon dillweed
2 teaspoons rosemary

1 teaspoon thyme
1 teaspoon basil
½ cup grated Parmesan
  cheese
2 tablespoons honey
1 egg
½ cup water

Preheat oven to 375°F.

In a large bowl, mix the ingredients in the order they are listed, using a large spoon or fork. When mixture clings together and no loose flour is evident, dough is ready to be baked.

If the batter is dry and you have trouble stirring, flour your hands and use them to press and knead the dough. If necessary, add a drop or two more of water. Shape dough into a loaf and place in a greased 9 x 5 x 3-inch loaf pan.

Bake 50 minutes. Test for doneness.

## • MAPLE BUTTERY MUFFINS •
8 minutes     1 dozen

1¾ cups unbleached flour
1 tablespoon baking powder
¼ teaspoon cinnamon
¼ cup vegetable oil
⅓ cup maple syrup

⅔ cup milk
1 egg
½ teaspoon vanilla or maple
  extract
½ cup chopped nuts

Preheat oven to 425°F.

Whisk together the first 3 ingredients.

Blend oil, maple syrup, milk, egg, and extract until mixture is

smooth. Add to dry ingredients and blend well. Fold in nuts.
Spoon batter into greased muffin tins.

Bake 15-20 minutes.

## • MOLASSES BREAD •

7 minutes    1 loaf

1½ cups unbleached flour       ½ cup plain yogurt
1½ cups whole wheat flour      1 tablespoon baking soda
¼ cup cornmeal                 ½ cup molasses

Preheat oven to 350°F.

Combine all the ingredients in a large bowl and stir with a large
spoon, or knead with floured hands until dough is blended. The
dough is well mixed when it clings together and leaves no loose
flour in the bowl. It might be necessary to add a few extra drops
of liquid to mix, but use sparingly. Pat dough into a greased 9 x
5 x 3-inch loaf pan.

Bake 50 minutes. Test for doneness.

## • POPOVERS •

5 minutes    1½ dozen

These crusty, hollow shells pop up while baking.

4 eggs                           2 cups unbleached flour
2 cups milk

Preheat oven to 450°F.

Beat eggs slightly. Stir in remaining ingredients just until the
batter is smooth. Do not overmix. Fill greased muffin cups three
quarters full.

Bake 25 minutes.

Lower oven temperature to 350°F. Bake 15-20 more minutes. Remove from the oven when popovers are golden brown. Remove from tins and serve hot. Spread with butter, fruit butters, nut butters, or cream cheese, if desired.

*Variation:*
CHEDDAR CHEESE POPOVERS—Add 2 cups of Cheddar cheese to the above recipe batter. Bake as directed.

## • PUMPKIN MUNCHKINS •
8 minutes    1 dozen

1½ cups unbleached flour
1 tablespoon baking powder
½ teaspoon cinnamon
½ teaspoon nutmeg
1 egg

½ cup milk
1 cup pumpkin puree
¼ cup vegetable oil
¼ cup honey
½ cup raisins

Preheat oven to 400°F.
Whisk the first 4 ingredients together in a large bowl.
Blend egg, milk, pumpkin puree, oil, and honey until mixture is smooth. Add to dry ingredients and blend until moistened. Fold in raisins. Spoon batter into greased muffin cups.
Bake 15-20 minutes.
Serve with nut butters, cottage or cream cheese, or fruit jams.

## • SUNSHINE BREAD •
8 minutes    1 loaf

This crumbly snack bread is good hot or cold anytime of the day. We especially like it with strawberry jam.

1 cup cornmeal
1 cup unbleached flour
2 teaspoons baking powder
¼ cup vegetable oil

¼ cup honey
1 cup milk
1 egg

Preheat oven to 425°F.
   In a large bowl, whisk the first 3 ingredients. Make a well in the center.
   Blend the remaining ingredients until the mixture is smooth. Add to the dry ingredients. Stir until batter is just moistened and still lumpy. Pour batter into a greased 8-inch square pan.
   Bake 20-25 minutes.

## • CRACKLING WHEAT MUFFINS •
7 minutes   1 dozen

1 cup unbleached flour
½ cup whole wheat flour
2 teaspoons baking powder
1 egg
½ cup milk

¼ cup vegetable oil
½ cup honey
½ teaspoon grated lemon peel
½ cup sunflower seeds

Preheat oven to 375°F.
   Whisk together the first 3 ingredients. Make a well in the center.
   Combine the remaining ingredients and add to dry mixture. Stir just until batter is blended but still lumpy. Fill greased muffin cups two-thirds full with batter.
   Bake 20 minutes. Remove from tins and cool.

## • QUICK WHOLE WHEAT BREAD •
7 minutes    1 loaf

1 cup whole wheat flour
1 cup unbleached flour
1 cup wheat germ, bran,
　chopped nuts, or seeds

1 tablespoon baking soda
2 tablespoons maple syrup
1 cup plain yogurt
1 egg

Preheat oven to 350°F.

In a large bowl, combine the ingredients in the order they are listed. Stir with a large spoon or fork, or press and knead with floured hands, until the mixture clings together and there is no loose flour in the bottom of the bowl. If necessary, add a few extra drops of liquid. Shape dough into a loaf and place in a greased loaf pan.

Bake 45 minutes. Test for doneness.

## • ZUCCHINI BREAD •
10 minutes    2 loaves

3 eggs
3 teaspoons vanilla extract
1 cup vegetable oil
½ cup raisins
1 cup chopped walnuts

2 cups grated zucchini
1⅓ cups honey
3 cups unbleached flour
1 teaspoon baking soda
2 teaspoons cinnamon

Preheat oven to 350°F.

Blend the first 7 ingredients until mixture is smooth.

Whisk flour, baking soda, and cinnamon. Add to wet mixture and stir until well blended. Pour mixture into 2 greased 9 x 5 x 3-inch loaf pans.

Bake 55-60 minutes. Test for doneness. Allow to cool before slicing.

# · Cookies and Crackers ·

Mention "cookie" and watch a child's face light up! Cookies are universally loved by kids, and almost as universally dismissed by moms and dads as nutritionally empty, sugar-laden, between-meal sweets that ruin appetites for good, nutritious meals.

Well, not anymore! We've changed all that by taking the guilt out of serving cookies. Our cookie recipes are not only good tasting, they are good for your kids.

You will surely recognize some of the names but, reading on, we think you'll be pleasantly surprised at the positive changes we've made to convert these old standbys into nutrient-rich, sugar-free additions to your children's diets.

We'd like to point out and quickly explain one of those changes. When baking cookies, you can choose to use oil or butter. Oil, an unsaturated fat, is better for your kids than butter, a saturated fat (see Introduction, page 2). These fats include safflower oil, corn oil, sunflower oil and soy oil. Many of us, however, love the rich melt-in-your-mouth goodness that only butter seems to give cookies. As a compromise to good nutrition and good taste, we recommend using Butter's Brother (page 14) in recipes that we think are enhanced by a buttery flavor. You may also substitute it in other recipes that call for either oil or butter and get the best of both foods.

Cookies can be prepared for baking in either of two ways. The traditional "teaspoon" method is to drop the dough by teaspoon-

85

fuls onto a cookie sheet. This method adds a few more minutes to the preparation time since you must repeatedly fill and empty cookie sheets and remove and replace them in the oven. Our preparation times don't reflect these extra few minutes.

A much faster way is to spread the dough in a square pan or a cookie sheet. Bake as usual, and when the cookies are completely cool, cut into bars. This is a real time-saver. Either way, the cookies taste great. It's just a matter of preference and how much time you have. After a little trial and error, you will decide which method is best for you.

## Some Tips

Use bright, shiny cookie sheets. Dark ones absorb heat and may overcook the cookie bottoms.

Cookie dough should always be placed on a cool sheet to prevent it from melting and spreading.

It saves time to use three or four cookie sheets, filling one or two while one or two more are in the oven.

A quick trick if you don't have enough cookie sheets is to cut aluminum foil to fit the pan(s) you do have. Place cookie dough on the foil. You will be able to slide the foil onto the warm cookie sheet and pop it right back into the oven.

Be careful not to overbake cookies.

Always remove cookies immediately from the warm sheet to a wire rack unless a recipe specifically states not to. A broad spatula is best to use.

Be sure cookies are thoroughly cool before storing.

Store cookies in an airtight container. Bar cookies can be covered and stored in the pan they were baked in.

Why not bake some giant cookies? It is amazing how an old favorite can take on a new zest for children just by becoming bigger.

## Freezing Cookies

Both baked and unbaked cookies may be frozen up to 12 months, if properly packaged. Be sure to mark the package clearly with the date and what it is.

*To Freeze Unbaked Cookies:* There are two ways to freeze unbaked cookies: (1) form dough into a bar shape and wrap tightly in aluminum foil or plastic wrap, or place in an airtight container and then in the freezer; (2) drop dough by teaspoonfuls onto a cookie sheet and place in the freezer. When hard, package the individual cookies in plastic bags or airtight containers and return to the freezer.

*To Thaw:* unwrap and allow dough to stand at room temperature until it can be handled easily.

*To Freeze Baked Cookies:* Allow cookies to cool completely and pack them in plastic bags. If they are very crunchy or delicate, arrange them on a cookie sheet and place in the freezer. Then repack in plastic bags when frozen.

## • BUTTER-CHEESE DELIGHTS •
8 minutes   3 dozen

½ cup Butter's Brother
  (page 14)
¼ cup cottage cheese
1 teaspoon vanilla extract
⅔ cup honey

1 egg
2 cups unbleached flour,
  whisked
½ teaspoon baking soda

Preheat oven to 350°F.

Blend the first 2 ingredients until smooth. Add vanilla, honey, and egg as you continue beating. Add remaining ingredients and mix well.

Drop batter by teaspoonfuls onto a greased cookie sheet.

Bake 10-12 minutes. Or spread batter evenly over a greased cookie sheet. Bake 12-15 minutes. Cool and cut into bars.

## • BUTTERSCOTCH BROWNIES •
10 minutes   2 dozen

¼ cup Butter's Brother
  (page 14)
½ cup vegetable oil
1 cup honey
½ cup molasses

3 eggs
1 teaspoon vanilla extract
2½ cups unbleached flour
3 teaspoons baking soda
¾ cup chopped nuts

Preheat oven to 350°F.
   Blend the first 5 ingredients until mixture is smooth. Add vanilla. Stir well.
   Whisk flour and baking soda. Add to wet mixture and blend well. Stir in nuts. Spread batter in a greased 9-inch square pan.
   Bake 20-25 minutes. Cool and cut into squares.

## • BUTTERSCOTCH-OATMEAL COOKIES •
10 minutes   3 dozen

¾ cup unbleached flour
½ cup noninstant dry milk
1½ cups wheat germ
2 cups rolled oats
½ cup raisins

¾ cup vegetable oil
1 cup honey
2 tablespoons molasses
2 teaspoons vanilla extract
2 eggs

Preheat oven to 350°F.
   Combine the first 5 ingredients. Mix well.
   Beat together the remaining ingredients until blended. Add to dry ingredients and stir until mixed. Spread batter evenly over a cookie sheet.
   Bake 20 minutes. Cool and cut into squares.

## • CAROB BROWNIES •

10 minutes   2½ dozen

¼ cup unbleached flour
1 cup peanuts
1 cup carob powder
1 cup vegetable oil

⅔ cup honey
4 eggs
2 teaspoons vanilla extract
1 cup mixed nuts and seeds

Preheat oven to 325°F.

Blend the first 3 ingredients in a blender or food processor until mixture is the consistency of flour.

Add oil, honey, eggs, and vanilla, and continue to blend.

Stir in mixed nuts and seeds. Spread mixture in a greased 9-inch square pan.

Bake 40 minutes. Cool and cut into squares.

## • CHEESE-BITS •

10 minutes   2-3 dozen

½ cup Butter's Brother
(page 14)
½ cup grated Parmesan
cheese

1 cup unbleached flour
½ teaspoon baking powder

Preheat oven to 425°F.

Beat together the first 2 ingredients.

Whisk flour and baking powder. Add to butter mixture. Roll dough out on a lightly floured surface and cut into 1-inch diameter rounds. Place on an ungreased cookie sheet.

Bake 8-10 minutes. Cool.

## • CHEESE TWISTS •

10 minutes    6 dozen

These freeze beautifully and are an absolute necessity to have on hand for snack time.

**2 cups unbleached flour**
**¼ teaspoon paprika**
**¾ cup Butter's Brother (page 14), softened**

**1½ cups shredded Cheddar cheese**
**⅓-½ cup cold water**

Preheat oven to 400°F.

Whisk together flour and paprika. Add Butter's Brother and beat until mixture is smooth and blended. Add cheese and enough water to form a smooth dough. Refrigerate at least ½ hour.

Roll dough out on a floured surface to ¼-inch thickness. Cut into ½ x 4-inch strips. Twist strips and place them on an ungreased cookie sheet.

Bake 10-12 minutes.

Or place cookie sheets directly into the freezer. When twists are frozen, remove to plastic bags or airtight containers and return to the freezer for later use. You need not thaw them before baking.

## • CHOCOLATE CHIP NUTTEROS •

10 minutes   3 dozen

1½ cups unbleached flour
½ teaspoon baking soda
1 egg
½ cup vegetable oil or Butter's
   Brother (page 14)

½ cup (scant) honey
1 teaspoon vanilla extract
½ cup carob chips
½ cup chopped nuts

Preheat oven to 350°F.

Whisk together the first 2 ingredients. Make a well and add egg, oil, honey, and vanilla. Mix well. Fold in carob chips and chopped nuts.

Drop mixture by teaspoonfuls, or spread mixture evenly over a cookie sheet.

Bake 10-12 minutes, or until cookies are fat and golden.

## • CORN CHIPS •

11 minutes   2 dozen

To toast cornmeal: place cornmeal in a shallow pan and bake in a 350°F. oven for 15 minutes. Always keep some on hand to sprinkle on toast, soups, or salads.

½ cup toasted yellow
   cornmeal
½ cup yellow cornmeal
⅓ cup unbleached flour
¼ teaspoon baking soda
⅛ teaspoon pepper

¾ teaspoon chili powder
½ cup plain yogurt
3 tablespoons vegetable oil
2 teaspoons coarse salt
   (optional)

Preheat oven to 350°F.

In a medium-size bowl, combine the first 6 ingredients. Blend yogurt and oil. Add to cornmeal mixture and stir until dough forms a ball. Knead with your hands until the dough is well mixed.

Roll into a square about ¼ inch thick. Sprinkle coarse salt over dough and roll a rolling pin lightly over to press the salt in. Cut into 1-inch squares. Place on a lightly oiled cookie sheet.

Bake 15 minutes, or until chips are lightly browned. Can be stored in an airtight container for several weeks.

### • CURLY-WURLYS •
5 minutes

We always whip these up with the dough scraps left over after making pies. But they are so popular with the kids, you might have to skip the pie!

**Your favorite pie crust recipe**          **Honey**
**Butter or Butter's Brother**              **Cinnamon**
  **(page 14)**

Roll dough out flat on a floured surface. Dot with butter and spread on a very thin coat of honey. Sprinkle with cinnamon.

Starting at one end, roll dough jelly-roll style. Cut rolled dough into slices, each about ½-inch thick. Place on a cookie sheet.

Bake in a 350°F. oven for 15-20 minutes.

*Variations:*

For an even faster treat; roll dough out on a cookie sheet, add toppings, and bake flat for 10 minutes. Allow cookies to cool before cutting.

Substitute shredded cheese for honey/butter mixture.

# • GINGERBREAD MEN •

7 minutes    4 dozen

Half the fun of these moist, plump cookies is letting the kids cut out the dough with their favorite cookie cutters. If you don't have the time or the helpers, you can spread the dough in a 13 x 9-inch pan and bake 15-20 minutes.

½ cup vegetable oil
½ cup molasses
¼ cup honey
½ cup milk
1 tablespoon plain yogurt
3½ cups unbleached flour

1½ teaspoons ground ginger
2 teaspoons baking powder
½ teaspoon baking soda
1 teaspoon lemon or orange
   extract or 1 teaspoon
   thawed juice concentrate

Preheat oven to 350°F.

Combine the first 5 ingredients until they are thoroughly blended.

Whisk together flour, ginger, baking powder, and baking soda. Add to wet mixture. Add extract and stir until a smooth dough is formed.

On a lightly floured surface, roll dough out to ⅓-inch thickness and cut with cookie cutters. Place on an ungreased cookie sheet.

Bake 8-10 minutes. Remove from pans to cool.

Decorate with Cream Cheese Frosting (page 118), coconut, dried fruit, peanuts, or raisins.

## • GRAHAM SCRAM COOKIES •
10 minutes   2-3 dozen

1 cup unbleached flour
1 cup whole wheat flour
1 teaspoon baking powder
¼ cup Butter's Brother
   (page 14)

¼ cup honey
¼ cup (scant) milk

Preheat oven to 400°F.

Whisk together the first 3 ingredients. Cut in Butter's Brother until mixture has a granular consistency. Add honey and mix. Add milk and mix again.

On a lightly floured surface, roll dough out to ¼-inch thickness. Cut into squares and place on an ungreased cookie sheet. Prick with a fork and brush with additional milk to assure golden color.

Bake 15-20 minutes. Remove from pan and allow to cool thoroughly.

## • GRANOLA GRABS •
7 minutes   2 dozen

2 cups unbleached flour
1 teaspoon baking soda
2 eggs
⅔ cup vegetable oil

⅔ cup honey
1 teaspoon vanilla extract
2½ cups granola

Preheat oven to 325°F.

Whisk flour and baking soda together. Make a well and add eggs, oil, honey, and vanilla. Mix well. Add granola and mix again.

Drop by teaspoonfuls or spread dough evenly over a greased cookie sheet.

Bake 10 minutes, or until golden brown around the edges.

## • HONEY-CHIP COOKIES •

### 7 minutes    6 dozen

1 cup plus 2 tablespoons
  unbleached flour
½ teaspoon baking soda
½ cup Butter's Brother
  (page 14)

¾ cup honey
1 egg
½ teaspoon vanilla extract
1 cup carob chips

Preheat oven to 350°F.
  Whisk the first 2 ingredients.
  Blend Butter's Brother and honey until fluffy. Add egg and vanilla and continue mixing until blended. Add mixture to dry ingredients. Stir until completely blended. Fold in carob chips.
  Drop by teaspoonfuls, about 2 inches apart, or spread dough evenly over a greased cookie sheet.
  Bake 10-12 minutes. Cool on racks.

## • HONEY-LEMON COOKIES •

### 6 minutes    3 dozen

This crispy cookie is good plain as a snack or lunchbox treat or it can be frosted and decorated for a party or holiday cookie. The kids will have fun cutting them into shapes.

½ cup Butter's Brother
  (page 14)
1 egg
½ cup honey

1 teaspoon lemon extract
2¾ cups unbleached flour

Preheat oven to 350°F.
  Mix the first 4 ingredients. Add flour and mix again until dough is smooth. Chill at least 1 hour.
  Roll chilled dough out on a floured surface and cut out with

your favorite cookie cutters, or use the lightly floured rim of a drinking glass.

Bake 10 minutes. Remove from pans to wire racks or wax paper immediately and allow to cool.

## • HONEY NUTTY DATE BARS •
### 10 minutes    3 dozen

These bar cookies are chock full of rich dates and crunchy nuts.

| | |
|---|---|
| **1½ cups unbleached flour, whisked** | **1¾ cups chopped dates** |
| **1 teaspoon baking powder** | **2 tablespoons ground ginger** |
| **1 cup chopped nuts** | **3 eggs** |
| | **1 cup honey** |

Preheat oven to 350°F.

Whisk the first 2 ingredients. Make a well in the center.

Combine nuts and dates. Mix 2 tablespoons of the flour mixture with ginger and toss with nuts and dates until they are coated.

Beat eggs until they are frothy. Stir in honey. Add to dry ingredients and stir until well blended. Fold in floured nuts and dates. Spread mixture in a greased 13 x 9-inch pan.

Bake 30-35 minutes. Test for doneness by pressing center lightly; it's ready when it springs back. Cool and cover.

For best results, allow covered cookies to mellow overnight. Then spread with Cream Cheese Frosting (page 118) and sprinkle with chopped nuts. Cut into bars.

## • NUT CLOUDS •
5 minutes    2 dozen

These light, airy creations are a sure-fire hit with kids of all ages.

**2 egg whites**
**⅔ cup honey**
**½ teaspoon vanilla extract**

**1 tablespoon unbleached flour**
**1 cup coarsely chopped**
   **walnuts**

Preheat oven to 325°F.
   Beat egg whites until they are stiff. Slowly drizzle in honey as you continue beating. Add vanilla and beat. Fold in flour and nuts. Drop mixture by teaspoonfuls onto a greased and lightly floured baking sheet.
   Bake 10 minutes.

## • OATMEAL COOKIES •
7 minutes    4 dozen

Fruit and/or nuts can be added after dough is mixed. This is convenient if one youngster likes plain cookies and another is partial to fruit- and nut-studded ones.

**1½ cups unbleached flour**
**½ teaspoon baking soda**
**1 teaspoon cinnamon**
**2 cups rolled oats**
**1 cup raisins or chopped nuts**
   **(or a mixture of both)**

**1 egg**
**¼ cup milk**
**⅓ cup vegetable oil or**
   **Butter's Brother (page 14)**
**½ cup honey**
**1 teaspoon vanilla extract**

Preheat oven to 325°F.
   Mix the first 3 ingredients. Add oats, raisins, and/or nuts and mix thoroughly.

Blend the remaining ingredients until the mixture is smooth and creamy. Add to dry ingredients and stir until blended. Drop by teaspoonfuls, or spread mixture evenly over a greased cookie sheet.

Bake 15-20 minutes.

## • OATMEAL DANDIES •
### 10 minutes    3 dozen

¾ cup peanut butter (the chunk style is best)
3 tablespoons vegetable oil or Butter's Brother (page 14)

¼ cup honey
1½ cups rolled oats
1 cup raisins
¼ cup sunflower seeds

Combine the first 3 ingredients in the top of a double boiler over hot water. Stir occasionally until mixture is smooth. Remove from the heat and stir in the remaining ingredients. Spread mixture evenly in a greased 9-inch square pan and chill until firm. Be sure to chill thoroughly (at least 1 hour) or dough will fall apart. Cut into squares.

## • PEANUT BUTTER COOKIES •
### 7 minutes    5 dozen

2½ cups unbleached flour
1 teaspoon baking powder
1½ teaspoons baking soda
1½ cups peanut butter
½ cup vegetable oil or Butter's Brother (page 14)

¾ cup honey
2 eggs
1 cup raisins, chopped nuts, or carob chips (optional)

Preheat oven to 350°F.

Whisk together the first 3 ingredients. Make a well and add peanut butter, oil, honey, and eggs. Beat until well blended. Add raisins, nuts, or carob, if desired. Drop batter by teaspoonfuls onto a lightly greased cookie sheet.

Bake 10-12 minutes. After removing from oven, flatten each cookie with a fork in a crisscross pattern. Remove to wire racks to cool.

## • PUMPKIN PUFFS •
7 minutes    4 dozen

½ cup vegetable oil or
  Butter's Brother (page 14)
⅔ cup honey
2 eggs
1 cup cooked pumpkin
2 cups unbleached flour
4 teaspoons baking powder

2½ teaspoons cinnamon
½ teaspoon nutmeg
¼ teaspoon ground ginger
1 cup raisins
1 cup pecans, walnuts and/or
  sunflower seeds (optional)

Preheat oven to 350°F.

Mix the first 4 ingredients thoroughly. Add the dry ingredients and blend well. Stir in raisins and nuts and/or seeds, if desired. Drop mixture by teaspoonfuls or spread evenly over a greased cookie sheet.

Bake 25 minutes. Cool on wire racks.

## • SESAME-GRAIN CRUNCHIES •
6 minutes   3-4 dozen

1 cup rolled oats
¼ cup bran
1 cup whole wheat flour
⅓ cup vegetable oil

1 tablespoon honey
½ cup water
¼ cup sesame seeds

Preheat oven to 350°F.

Grind oats in a blender or food processor until they are the consistency of coarse flour. Add bran and whole wheat flour and blend.

Combine oil, honey, and water. Pour into dry ingredients and mix well. Pat dough out on a greased cookie sheet and roll with a rolling pin to ⅛-inch thickness. Sprinkle with sesame seeds and roll again to press seeds into dough. Using a sharp knife, mark dough into squares. Do not cut through dough entirely.

Bake 10-12 minutes. Remove crackers from pan immediately after taking them out of the oven. Cool on wire racks. Break along marked lines before storing.

## • SESAME SURPRISES •
7 minutes   3 dozen

1 cup shredded unsweetened
  coconut
¾ cup sesame seeds
1 egg
⅓ cup vegetable oil
¾ cup honey

2 cups unbleached flour
1 teaspoon vanilla extract
½ teaspoon baking powder
⅛ teaspoon baking soda
½ teaspoon cinnamon
¼ teaspoon ground cloves

Preheat oven to 300°F.

Mix coconut and seeds. Place in a pan and brown in oven, about 3 minutes.

Blend egg, oil, and honey. Add flour and stir. Add remaining ingredients. Mix well. Stir in toasted coconut and seeds. Drop by teaspoonfuls or spread mixture evenly over greased cookie sheets.

Bake 15-18 minutes. Remove to wire racks and cool.

## • YOGURT DELIGHTS •
8 minutes    4 dozen

⅔ cup vegetable oil or
  Butter's Brother (page 14)
¾ cup honey
1 teaspoon vanilla extract
2 eggs
2½ cups unbleached flour

1 teaspoon baking powder
2 teaspoons baking soda
1 cup plain yogurt
½ cup raisins
½ cup chopped walnuts

Preheat oven to 350°F.

Blend the first 3 ingredients. Add the eggs, one at a time, and beat well after each one.

Whisk the flour, baking powder, and baking soda. Alternately add the dry mixture and yogurt to honey mixture. Fold in the raisins and nuts. Drop by teaspoonfuls or spread mixture evenly over an ungreased cookie sheet.

Bake 12-15 minutes or longer.

## • WALDORF WAFERS •
### 7 minutes    4 dozen

1 cup honey
¾ cup mayonnaise
2 eggs
1 teaspoon vanilla extract
2¾ cups unbleached flour
½ teaspoon baking soda

1 teaspoon cinnamon
1½ cups apple, chunked but
   not peeled
1 cup chopped walnuts
¼ cup chopped celery

Preheat oven to 350°F.

Blend the first 4 ingredients. Add flour, baking soda, and cinnamon and blend until mixture is smooth. Stir in the remaining ingredients. Drop mixture by teaspoonfuls or spread evenly on an ungreased cookie sheet.

Bake 10-12 minutes. Remove from pan and cool on wire racks.

## • WHOLE WHEAT CRACKERS •
8 minutes   3-4 dozen

These solid, wholesome crackers are great with dips and spreads. They also make good travelers because they don't crumble easily.

1 cup rolled oats
½ cup whole wheat flour
½ cup unbleached flour

¼ cup wheat germ
½ cup water
¾ cup vegetable oil

Preheat oven to 350°F.

Whisk together the first 4 ingredients. Mix water and oil. Add to dry ingredients and blend well. Roll or pat dough out thick on a floured surface. Cut into squares and place on ungreased cookie sheets.

Bake 25-30 minutes.

*Variation:*

Sprinkle with sesame seeds before baking.

# · Cakes and Frostings ·

Cake has always been a favorite snack and the high point of many special occasions. Isn't it what you immediately think of to celebrate a new baby, a birthday, your daughter's soccer team's victorious season, or your son's Cub Scout banquet? Whether it's for a specific event or just because you feel like it, a cake is festive, happy, and fun.

Our recipes range from simple snacking cakes that your kids just won't be able to resist to light, airy creations that will do you proud at any affair.

The frosting recipes add a not-too-sweet finishing touch.

We test our cakes for doneness by inserting a toothpick into the center of the cake. If it comes out clean and dry, the cake is done. If batter or soft crumbs stick to the toothpick, bake a few minutes longer and test again.

## Freezing Cakes

Allow cakes and cupcakes to cool completely before freezing.

Wrap properly to ensure maximum protection up to 5 months. Use either aluminum foil or plastic wrap.

We don't recommend freezing frosted cakes.

We prefer not to freeze cake batter although it can be done.

For easier handling, place cake on a pan covered with wax

paper in the freezer. When frozen, remove and wrap properly and carefully. Replace in freezer.

Cut the cake into individual child-size pieces before freezing. It takes less time to freeze and thaw.

To thaw, allow wrapped cake to stand at room temperature for several hours.

## Freezing Frostings

Frostings may be frozen although most can be stored in the refrigerator much more satisfactorily up to 2 weeks.

Whipped cream freezes very well (up to two months). Place individual dollops on wax paper and freeze. When hard, repack in an airtight container and return to the freezer until needed.

## • ONE-PAN APPLE CAKE •

5 minutes

This yummy snack cake can be made quickly in one pan.

¼ cup vegetable oil
½ cup honey
1 cup unbleached flour
½ cup apple, chunked but not peeled

½ cup chopped nuts
1 egg
1 teaspoon baking powder
1 teaspoon vanilla extract
¼ teaspoon cinnamon

Preheat oven to 350°F.

Put all ingredients into an ungreased 8-inch square pan and mix well. Spread mixture evenly in pan.

Bake 25-30 minutes. Test for doneness. Allow cake to cool before cutting and serving from pan.

## • GRANDMA RAMM'S APPLESAUCE CAKE •

12 minutes

This excellent cake is so rich that the top browns before it is thoroughly baked. Be sure to test carefully for doneness.

¼ cup vegetable oil
⅓ cup honey
1 egg
¾ cup applesauce
1¼ cups unbleached flour,
  whisked
¼ teaspoon each: allspice,
  ground cloves, cinnamon

½ cup raisins
¼ cup chopped walnuts
  (optional)
1 teaspoon baking soda
¼ cup boiling water

Preheat oven to 350°F.

In a large bowl, blend the first 4 ingredients.

Whisk together flour and spices. Mix 2 tablespoons of flour mixture with raisins and nuts. Set aside.

Dissolve baking soda in boiling water.

Alternately add flour mixture and soda/water to applesauce mixture. Blend well after each addition. Fold in floured raisins and nuts. Scrape batter into a greased and floured 9-inch square pan.

Bake 50 minutes. Test for doneness. Cool and frost with Cream Cheese Frosting, if desired (page 118).

## • FAVORITE BASIC CAKE •
12 minutes

1½ cups honey
¾ cup butter or Butter's
  Brother (page 14)
4 eggs
3 cups unbleached flour,
  whisked

¼ teaspoon baking soda
3 teaspoons baking powder
¾ cup milk
1 teaspoon vanilla or lemon
  extract
2 teaspoons orange juice

Preheat oven to 375°F.

Beat honey and butter until creamed. Add eggs and continue beating until thoroughly blended.

Whisk together flour, baking powder, and baking soda. Alternately add the flour mixture and milk to butter mixture. Blend until smooth. Stir in extract and orange juice. Pour batter into two greased and floured 8- or 9-inch round pans.

Bake 20-30 minutes. Test for doneness. Cool in pans for 10 minutes before turning out on racks. Frost with your favorite frosting recipe.

## • CAROB NUT CAKE •
12 minutes

It is not necessary to separate the eggs. Whole eggs can be mixed in with wet ingredients if you are in a pinch for time. We must warn you, though, the cake will not be as light or as high.

2 cups unbleached flour
⅔ cup carob powder
2 teaspoons baking powder
1¼ teaspoons cinnamon
4 eggs, separated

1 cup milk
1 cup vegetable oil
⅔ cup honey
2½ teaspoons vanilla extract
½ cup chopped walnuts

Preheat oven to 350°F.

In a bowl, mix the first 4 ingredients.

Blend egg yolks, milk, oil, honey, and vanilla. Mix with dry ingredients until mixture is smooth.

Beat egg whites until stiff and fold them into batter. Fold in nuts. Pour batter into greased 13 x 9-inch pan.

Bake 35 minutes. Test for doneness. Frost with Honey-Nut Frosting (page 118).

## • CARROT CAKE •
### 10 minutes

| | |
|---|---|
| 1 cup vegetable oil | 2 teaspoons baking powder |
| 1 cup honey | 1½ teaspoons baking soda |
| 2 tablespoons orange juice | 2 teaspoons cinnamon |
| 4 eggs | 2 cups grated raw carrots |
| ½ cup water | ½ cup raisins |
| 3 cups unbleached flour | ½ cup chopped walnuts |

Preheat oven to 350°F.

Combine the first 5 ingredients and blend thoroughly.

Whisk flour, baking powder, baking soda, and cinnamon together. Add to wet mixture. Blend well. Stir in carrots, raisins, and nuts. Pour batter into a greased 10-inch tube pan.

Bake 30-45 minutes. Test for doneness.

## • COCONUT CAKE •
8 minutes

3 cups unbleached flour
2 teaspoons baking soda
1 cup vegetable oil
1 cup honey

2 cups plain yogurt
1½ cups shredded
   unsweetened coconut

Preheat oven to 350°F.

Whisk flour and baking soda together. Make a well in the center. Add oil and honey and blend until smooth. Add yogurt and coconut. Mix well after each addition. Spread batter in a greased 13 x 9-inch pan.

Bake 30-45 minutes. Test for doneness.

## • CONNIE'S CHEESECAKE •
15 minutes

This recipe is a variation of Jan's mom's favorite—but sugar-laden and time-consuming—dessert. We've adapted it to make it healthy, fast, and still delicious.

1 cup cream cheese, chunked
2 eggs
⅓ cup honey

1 teaspoon vanilla extract
9-inch baked pie shell

Preheat oven to 300°F.

Blend the first 4 ingredients until smooth. Pour mixture into pie shell.

Bake 20 minutes. Allow to cool before adding topping.

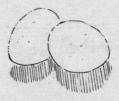

## Topping

**1 cup plain yogurt**
**1 tablespoon honey**

**1 teaspoon vanilla extract**

Reduce oven to 275°F.

Whisk ingredients in a small bowl. (Don't use a blender or food processor or topping will be too runny.) Spread on top of cheesecake.

Bake 10 minutes. Cool and refrigerate for 24 hours for maximum flavor—if you have the willpower to wait.

## • DEVIL'S FOOD CAKE •
### 7 minutes

**½ cup carob powder**
**1½ cups unbleached flour**
**1 teaspoon baking soda**
**2 eggs**
**¾ cup vegetable oil**

**⅔ cup honey**
**⅔ cup molasses**
**¾ cup milk**
**1 teaspoon vanilla extract**

Preheat oven to 350°F.

Whisk the first 3 ingredients.

Blend the remaining ingredients and add to dry ingredients; mix thoroughly. Pour batter into a 13 x 9-inch pan.

Bake 35-40 minutes. Test for doneness.

*Variation:*

Pour batter into muffin cups. Bake 15 minutes. Makes about 20 cupcakes.

## • DARK AND RICH GINGER CAKE •
### 7 minutes

3 cups unbleached flour
1 tablespoon ground ginger
2 teaspoons baking soda
2 teaspoons cinnamon
½ cup vegetable oil

½ cup honey
4 eggs
1 cup molasses
1 cup cold water
2 cups shredded coconut

Preheat oven to 350°F.

Whisk together the first 4 ingredients. Make a well in the center.

Blend oil, honey, eggs, and molasses until smooth. Add to dry ingredients and mix thoroughly. Stir in cold water and coconut. Pour into a greased 13 x 9-inch pan.

Bake 30-45 minutes. Test for doneness. Cool 10 minutes; then remove cake to wire rack and allow to cool completely. Serve with whipped cream.

## • GOLDEN HONEY CAKE •
### 8 minutes

2½ cups unbleached flour,
  whisked
1½ teaspoons baking soda
¾ teaspoon cinnamon
½ teaspoon nutmeg

¼ teaspoon allspice
½ cup vegetable oil
1 cup honey
1 egg
1 cup hot water

Preheat oven to 350°F.

Combine the first 5 ingredients and whisk.

Beat oil and honey until blended. Add egg and beat again. Add flour mixture to egg mixture and stir just until blended. Pour in hot water and beat until smooth. Pour batter into a greased 13 x 9-inch pan.

Bake 35-40 minutes. Test for doneness. Cool.

## • HONEY AND SPICE CUPCAKES •

8 minutes   1½ dozen

| | |
|---|---|
| 2½ cups unbleached flour | ½ cup honey |
| 2 teaspoons baking powder | 2 eggs |
| ½ cup vegetable oil | ⅔ cup milk |

Preheat oven to 350°F.

Combine all ingredients until mixture is thoroughly blended. Divide batter and place half in another bowl and add:

| | |
|---|---|
| 2 tablespoons molasses | ½ teaspoon nutmeg |
| 1 teaspoon cinnamon | 2 teaspoons ground cloves |

Mix thoroughly into batter. Spoon "yellow" and "spice" batters alternately into greased muffin cups. Or use a thin-bladed knife and swirl it through the batter to create a marbled effect.

Bake 10-12 minutes. Test for doneness.

*Variation:*

HONEY AND SPICE CAKE—Pour batter into a greased 9-inch square pan. Swirl a thin-bladed knife through batter to create a marbled effect. Bake at 350°F. for 15-20 minutes.

## • LEMON DREAM •
### 7 minutes

The easy Lemon Sauce is a cinch to make (it takes only 30 seconds) and tastes super. It is just as good on other plain cakes too.

1½ cups unbleached flour
1 teaspoon baking powder
¼ cup vegetable oil
¾ cup honey

2 eggs
⅔ cup plain yogurt
1 teaspoon vanilla extract
2 tablespoons lemon juice

Preheat oven to 350°F.
Whisk the flour and baking powder together.
Beat the remaining ingredients until mixture is blended smooth. Add to dry ingredients and stir until thoroughly blended. Pour batter into a greased 9 x 5 x 3-inch loaf pan.
Bake 50 minutes. Pour Lemon Sauce (below) over cake while it is still warm and in the pan.

*Variation:*
BLUEBERRY-LEMON DREAM—Add ½ cup of fresh or frozen blueberries to the Lemon Dream batter. Bake as directed.

## • LEMON SAUCE •
### 30 seconds

⅓ cup honey

1 tablespoon lemon juice

Blend honey and juice together. Pour over your favorite cake.

## • MAPLE-SPICE CAKE •
### 7 minutes

1½ cups unbleached flour
1 teaspoon baking soda
½ teaspoon ground ginger
1 teaspoon cinnamon

¼ cup vegetable oil
½ cup maple syrup
½ cup plain yogurt
1 egg

Preheat oven to 350°F.

In a large bowl, whisk the first 4 ingredients and make a well in the center. Add the remaining ingredients and mix thoroughly. Pour batter into a greased 8-inch square pan.

Bake 30-35 minutes. Test for doneness. Cool and cut and serve cake directly from pan. Top with whipped cream, if desired.


## • PINEAPPLE UPSIDE-DOWN CAKE •
### 8 minutes

Fresh pineapple can be used if you and your children prefer it.

½ cup vegetable oil
1 cup honey
2 eggs
2 cups unbleached flour
3 teaspoons baking soda
½ cup milk

4 tablespoons butter or
  Butter's Brother (page 14)
⅓ cup maple syrup
6 slices canned pineapple,
  drained

Preheat oven to 350°F.

Blend the first 3 ingredients until mixture is smooth.

Whisk flour and baking soda until light. Add alternately with milk to wet ingredients. Blend until smooth.

Put butter in a 9-inch square pan and place in oven until butter melts. Stir in maple syrup and arrange pineapple slices so that they are lying flat in the pan. Pour cake batter over them.

Bake 20-25 minutes. Test for doneness. Turn cake out onto a dish.

## • SAUCY NUT CAKE •
### 10 minutes

¼ cup vegetable oil
½ cup peanut butter
⅔ cup honey
1 cup applesauce
1 egg
1 cup unbleached flour

1 teaspoon baking soda
½ teaspoon cinnamon
¼ teaspoon nutmeg
½ cup pecans, walnuts, or
    sunflower seeds (optional)

Preheat oven to 350°F.
    Put the first 5 ingredients into a greased 9-inch square pan and mix well. Sprinkle dry ingredients over wet and mix again.
    Bake 30 minutes. Cool on a rack and serve right from the pan.

*Variations:*
    Add a small apple, chunked.
    Use chunky peanut butter for texture.

## • BUSY BAKEQUICK SHORTCAKES •
### 5 minutes    8 shortcakes

2 cups Busy Bakequick (page
    20)
½ cup vegetable oil
1 egg

¼ cup honey
¾ cup milk

Preheat oven to 400°F.
    Mix all ingredients thoroughly. Divide dough into 8 portions and spoon onto a greased cookie sheet.
    Bake 20-25 minutes.

*Variation:*

For an even faster shortcake, spread dough into a greased 8-inch round pan. Bake at 425°F. for 15-20 minutes.

## • SHORT-CUT SHORTCAKES •
5 minutes    Serves 4

**4 Busy Bakequick Shortcakes**          **Whipped cream**
**(page 116)**
**1 16-ounce can unsweetened**
**peaches**

Place opened can of peaches in a saucepan of hot water and warm over low heat.

Split shortcakes and spread with butter, if desired. Spoon hot peaches and juice over shortcakes. Top with whipped cream.

*Variations:*

Substitute 1 20-ounce can of crushed or chunked pineapple, warmed.

Heat a favorite jam or jelly and pour over cake; strawberry or raspberry jam, or orange marmalade is good.

Warm fresh or frozen blueberries, raspberries, or strawberries in a saucepan over low heat, crushing berries slightly as you stir, and pour over cake.

## • CREAM CHEESE FROSTING •
2 minutes   1 cup

This recipe works well on many snacks, cakes, and cookies, but we particularly recommend it on Honey Nutty Date Bars (page 146).

**1 cup cream cheese, softened**          **2 tablespoons honey**

Beat ingredients until mixture is smooth.

## • HONEY-NUT FROSTING •
5 minutes   1½ cups

**1 cup cream cheese**            **1¼ teaspoons vanilla extract**
**3 tablespoons honey**          **¼ cup chopped nuts**
**½ cup shredded coconut**

Beat cream cheese until fluffy. Add remaining ingredients and beat until mixture is smooth.

*Variation:*
   Substitute almond or lemon extract for vanilla extract.

## • QUICK HONEY FROSTING •

5 minutes    1 cup

This recipe can be doubled or tripled if necessary.

1 cup honey                              ½ cup shredded coconut
½ cup chopped nuts

Warm honey slightly until it is spreadable. Stir in nuts and coconut. Spread frosting gently on cake.

## • MERINGUE •

5 minutes

2 egg whites                             ½ teaspoon cream of tartar
1-2 tablespoons honey

Beat egg whites until thick and creamy. Gradually add honey while continuing to beat. When meringue forms stiff peaks, beat in cream of tartar.

When spreading meringue on top of a pie, make sure to seal it to the crust around the edges. This prevents the meringue from shrinking.

Pop the pie into a 425°F. oven for 5 minutes, or until meringue is lightly browned.

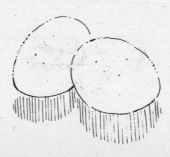

## • MOCHA FROSTING •
10 minutes    1¼ cups

½ cup Super Syrup (page 14)                    1 cup sour cream
4 tablespoons honey

Combine the first 2 ingredients in a saucepan. Simmer over low heat, stirring constantly, for about 6 minutes. Remove from heat and allow to cool slightly. Stir in sour cream until it is blended.


## • WHIPPED CREAM OUR WAY •
5 minutes    1 cup

1 cup heavy cream                              2 tablespoons honey

Beat cream until it begins to stiffen. Fold in honey. Serve immediately or chill. Store in the refrigerator.

# · Pies and Puddings ·

Pie is at the top of the popularity polls when it comes to snacks. Everyone has a favorite kind—apple, blueberry, custard, lemon meringue, pumpkin—and the list can go on and on. But everyone will agree that the one special ingredient that all good pies must have is a tender, flaky crust. Most people shy away from making pies because they feel that pie crust is a real challenge. However, with just a little practice and some good sound advice, anyone can succeed.

If you don't have the time or the inclination to tackle making your own pie crust, some excellent brands of frozen pie shells are available in most grocery stores. We have found several in our area that are great-tasting and contain not one iota of artificial ingredients or preservatives. Just read the labels carefully before buying.

Some of the pudding recipes included here can double as pie fillings when plopped into a baked pie shell. But don't limit them to that; these puddings can hold their own in the snack polls.

## Some Tips

Always handle crust carefully and gently. This keeps the air in the pastry and prevents it from becoming tough.

Be sure to use ice-cold water when making pastry. Drop a few ice cubes in a measuring cup and cover with water before starting to prepare pastry.

Add water, a tablespoon at a time, and toss crust with a fork after each addition.

Press dough into a firm ball with your hands after it is thoroughly mixed.

Roll dough out into a circle on a floured surface. Lift it occasionally to prevent it from sticking. We find a broad spatula works best.

For easier handling, fold pastry into quarters and lift it gently into the pie pan; then unfold.

If you need only one crust, why not double the recipe? You can put the extra crust in another pie pan and freeze it. Just a little more time now will save you a lot of time later.

*To store:* Keep pies and puddings in the refrigerator. If they are going to be there more than a day or two, you might want to cover them so they won't absorb other food flavors. This is especially true of cream-based pies and puddings.

## Freezing Pies

Pie shells can be frozen either unbaked or baked.

*Unbaked* will keep up to 2 months. There is no need to thaw them. You can pop them right into the oven still frozen.

*Baked* will keep up to 4 months. To thaw, unwrap and let stand at room temperature. Or place in 350°F. oven for 5 minutes if you are in a hurry.

Cool baked pies completely before freezing.

Bake fruit pies before freezing.

We don't recommend freezing cream, custard, or meringue pies.

To package freezer-bound pies properly, freeze them, then remove from the freezer and wrap in plastic wrap or bags, aluminum foil, or airtight containers. Firmly sealed, secured, and labeled and dated clearly, baked pies will keep up to 6 months. To thaw, allow pies to stand unwrapped at room temperature for 2-3 hours.

## • BASIC PIE CRUST •
8 minutes

Enough dough for either an 8- or 9-inch pie.

*1 single crust*

**1 cup plus 2 tablespoons
unbleached flour**
**⅓ cup vegetable oil**
**2-3 tablespoons ice water**

*1 double crust*

**1¾ cups flour**
**½ cup oil**
**3-4 tablespoons ice water**

Measure flour into a bowl. Add oil and mix with a fork until mixture is well blended. Add ice water, 1 tablespoon at a time, until a firm ball is formed and dough cleans the sides of the bowl. Gather dough (or half the dough if you are making a double crust) and shape into a flattened round. Roll out on a floured surface with a well-floured rolling pin until dough is 2 inches larger than pie pan. Fold pastry into quarters to pick up more easily. Ease into pan and unfold.

For a 1-crust pie, trim overhanging edge of pastry about 1 inch from edge of pan. Fold pastry under evenly and flute. Fill and bake as directed in recipe.

To bake an "empty" pie shell, prick bottom and sides of pie crust thoroughly with a fork before baking in a 475°F. oven for 12-15 minutes.

For a 2-crust pie, line pie pan with one of the rolled crusts and trim as above for a 1-crust pie. Do not fold edge under. Fill with desired filling. Roll out second ball of dough; fold into quarters and place over filling; unfold. Trim excess edge of pastry. Fold and roll top edge under lower edge. Press two layers together on pan rim to seal and flute.

It is important to remember to cut slits in top crust of pie to allow steam to escape and prevent pie filling from spilling over while baking.

To get even more goodies from your endeavors, make Curly Wurlys (page 92), cookies you can make with leftover pie dough. They are fast, easy, and your kids will love you for them.

## • CRUMB CRUST •
### 5 minutes

The Graham Scram Cookies (page 94) are tasty and can be ground quickly into crumbs. Or, if you prefer, there are many fine commercial products available.

|                          | *8-inch pie crust* | *9-inch pie crust* |
|--------------------------|--------------------|--------------------|
| Graham cracker crumbs    | 1¼ cups            | 1⅓ cups            |
| Honey                    | 2 tablespoons      | 3 tablespoons      |
| Butter, melted           | 3 tablespoons      | ¼ cup              |

Preheat oven to 350°F.

Mix all ingredients thoroughly. Press mixture firmly and evenly against pie plate bottom and sides. The easiest way to do this is to place another pie pan into the crumb mixture pan and press down.

Bake 8-10 minutes. Cool.

## • GROUND NUT CRUST •
### 5 minutes

| | |
|---|---|
| 1½ cups ground almonds, pecans, peanuts, or walnuts | 1½ tablespoons honey<br>2 tablespoons butter |

Preheat oven to 400°F.

Blend ingredients with your fingers until well mixed. Press mixture firmly into a lightly buttered 9-inch pie pan.

Bake 6-8 minutes. Cool before filling.

## • TART SHELLS •
10 minutes    1½-2 dozen

Fill these miniature pastry shells with a multitude of delicious fillings for any occasion.

Preheat oven to 475°F.

Make Basic Pie Crust (page 123).

Roll dough into a 12-inch circle about ⅛-inch thick.

Cut out 4½-inch diameter round of dough using a cutter or the rim of a drinking glass.

Fit the "rounds" over the back of muffin cups, making pleats if necessary so pastry fits close. Prick with a fork to prevent excessive puffiness.

Bake 8-10 minutes. Cool thoroughly before removing from the back of muffin cups.

## • APPLE PIE •
10 minutes

If you like your pie sweeter, vary honey accordingly.

*pastry for an 8-inch, 2 crust pie*

**5 cups apples, peeled and cut into thin slices**
**⅓ cup honey**
**3 tablespoons unbleached flour**
**¼ teaspoon nutmeg**
**¼ teaspoon cinnamon**
**1 tablespoon butter or Butter's Brother (page 14)**

*pastry for a 9-inch, 2-crust pie*

**6 cups apples, peeled and cut into thin slices**
**½ cup honey**
**¼ cup unbleached flour**
**½ teaspoon nutmeg**
**½ teaspoon cinnamon**
**2 tablespoons butter or Butter's Brother**

Preheat oven to 425°F.

Drizzle honey over sliced apples in a bowl.

Mix flour and spices together. Toss with honeyed apple slices until they are well coated. Set aside.

Line pie pan with pie crust. If you are using a frozen pie shell, you can fill the bottom crust while it is still frozen. The top crust should be thawed, however, to allow for easier handling. Turn fruit into pastry-lined pan and dot with butter. Cover with top crust. Seal and flute. Cut slits in top crust to allow steam to escape. Cover pie edges with aluminum foil strips to prevent excessive browning. Remove strips the last 15 minutes of baking.

Bake 40-50 minutes, or until juice bubbles through slits in top and crust is golden brown.

## • BANANA BLISS PIE •
### 10 minutes

One mouthful will convince you there is no other name for it.

*Crust:*

¼ cup coconut
¼ cup sesame seeds
¾ cup rolled oats
¼ cup vegetable oil

¼ cup honey
¼ cup sunflower seeds
¼ cup unbleached flour
½ teaspoon vanilla extract

Combine all of the ingredients until they are just blended. Don't overdo it. Pat mixture into a greased 9-inch round pan.

*Filling:*

6 bananas
3 eggs
¾ cup honey

½ cup milk
1 teaspoon vanilla extract
1¼ cups light cream

Preheat oven to 300°F.

Blend all ingredients until smooth and creamy. Pour mixture over crust.

Bake 60 minutes, or until a thin knife inserted comes out clean. Serve with whipped cream, if desired.

## • BLUEBERRY PIE •
10 minutes

Pastry for an 8-inch, 2-crust pie

¼ cup honey
¼ cup unbleached flour
½ teaspoon cinnamon
  (optional)

3 cups fresh blueberries,
  cleaned and picked over
1 teaspoon lemon juice
1 tablespoon butter

Preheat oven to 425°F.
  Blend honey, flour, and cinnamon. Mix with berries.
  Pour fruit into a pastry-lined pan. Sprinkle with lemon juice and dot with butter. Cover with top crust; seal and flute edges. Cover edges with aluminum foil strips to prevent excessive browning. Remove these the last 15 minutes of baking.
  Bake 35-45 minutes, or until juice bubbles through top and crust is brown.


## • BROWNIE PIE •
8 minutes

4 eggs
⅓ cup honey
1 teaspoon vanilla extract
1 cup cream cheese

½ cup carob powder
½ cup chopped peanuts
  (optional)
9-inch unbaked pie shell

Preheat oven to 350°F.
  Blend the first 5 ingredients until mixture is smooth. Stir in chopped peanuts, if desired. Pour mixture into pie shell.
  Bake 40-45 minutes. Allow to cool before serving.

## • CHEESE PIE •
10 minutes

2 cups ricotta cheese
⅓ cup honey
4 eggs, lightly beaten

½ teaspoon vanilla extract
9-inch unbaked pie shell

Preheat oven to 325°F.
Blend the first 4 ingredients until smooth. Pour into pie shell.
Bake 25 minutes. Remove from oven.

### Topping

1 cup plain yogurt
1 tablespoon warm water

½ teaspoon vanilla extract

Increase oven temperature to 425°F.
Combine yogurt, water, and vanilla. Spread mixture on top of
pie.
Bake 5 minutes. Cool.

## • COCONUT CUSTARD PIE •
5 minutes

4 eggs
⅓ cup honey
2½ cups milk
1 teaspoon vanilla extract

½ cup shredded unsweetened
coconut
9-inch unbaked pie shell

Preheat oven to 425°F.
Blend the first 4 ingredients until smooth. Stir in coconut. Pour
mixture into pie shell.
Bake 30 minutes, or until a thin knife inserted 1 inch from edge
of pie comes out clean. Sprinkle additional coconut on top, if
desired.

## • CONTINENTAL CHEESECAKE PIE •
10 minutes

⅓ cup honey
1 cup cream cheese, chunked
4 eggs
1½ teaspoons vanilla extract

½ teaspoon lemon juice
½ cup mixed nuts and seeds
9-inch unbaked pie shell

Preheat oven to 350°F.
   Blend the first 5 ingredients until smooth. Add nuts and seeds and mix well. Pour mixture into pie shell.
   Bake 40-45 minutes. Cool before serving.

## • HONEYED WALNUT PIE •
6 minutes

2 eggs
1 cup honey
1 teaspoon vanilla extract
1 tablespoon butter, chunked

1 tablespoon unbleached flour
1 cup chopped walnuts
8-inch unbaked pie shell

Preheat oven to 375°F.
   Beat eggs lightly. Add the next 3 ingredients and continue beating. Add flour and beat again. Stir in walnuts. Pour mixture into pie shell.
   Bake 40-50 minutes. Test by inserting a thin-bladed knife into the center. When it comes out clean, pie is done. Serve cold.

*Variation:*
   Substitute pecans for walnuts.

## • APRICOT MOUSSE •
12 minutes   Serves 6

1 cup dried apricots
⅔ cup water
¼ cup honey

1 cup whipping cream
1½ tablespoons orange juice
½ teaspoon vanilla

In a small saucepan, combine the first 3 ingredients and bring to a boil; reduce heat and simmer, uncovered, about 10 minutes.

While apricot mixture is cooking, beat whipping cream until stiff. Place in the refrigerator.

Puree apricot mixture in a blender or food processor. Add orange juice and extract; stir well. Fold whipped cream into mixture.

Spoon into individual dishes and chill.

## • BANANA CARAMEL •
8 minutes   Serves 4

¼ cup butter
1 cup maple syrup
1 cup whipping cream

1 tablespoon vanilla extract
6 bananas, slightly mashed

Melt butter in saucepan. Stir in maple syrup and cook over medium-low heat for about 5 minutes.

Whip cream until it is stiff. Stir in extract.

Add bananas to maple/butter syrup. Stir well. Fold in whipped cream. Spoon caramel into tall glasses and chill before serving.

## • BREAD PUDDING •
### 7 minutes    Serves 4

3 slices whole wheat bread
  (approx. 3 cups), chunked
2 tablespoons vegetable oil
¼ cup honey

1½ cups milk
2 eggs
1 teaspoon vanilla extract
Nutmeg (optional)

Preheat oven to 350°F.

Place bread chunks in a 1½-quart ovenproof bowl or baking dish.

Blend the next 5 ingredients until smooth. Pour mixture over bread chunks. Stir. Sprinkle with nutmeg.

Set dish in a larger size pan. Pour in hot water until it is halfway up the sides of the baking dish.

Bake 45 minutes, or until pudding is set. After removing bowl from oven, stir well. (You can throw in a handful of raisins at this time if you'd like. Just stir them in.) Serve pudding warm or chilled.

## • STOVE-TOP CHEESE CUPS •
### 7 minutes    Serves 4

½ cup shredded Cheddar
  cheese
1 tablespoon chives or
  chopped onion

4 eggs
2 cups milk
⅛ teaspoon pepper

Evenly divide cheese and chives or onion among 4 10-ounce baking cups or ovenproof dishes.

Beat remaining ingredients until smooth. Divide mixture evenly among cups.

Place cups in a large skillet and pour hot water in up to the level of the custard mixture. Cover pan with a tight-fitting lid and bring slowly to a boil. Turn heat off and let stand 15 minutes. Serve hot.

Leftovers can be served cold later.

*Variation:*

Sprinkle with shredded coconut, dried fruits, gorp, granola, or chopped nuts and seeds.

## • BAKED CUSTARD •
5 minutes   Serves 4

2 eggs
4 tablespoons honey
2 cups milk

1 teaspoon vanilla extract
Nutmeg

Preheat oven to 350°F.

Beat eggs until they are foamy. Add remaining ingredients and continue beating until blended. Pour mixture into 4 individual baking cups. Sprinkle with nutmeg.

Set dishes in a large pan. Pour in hot water until it is halfway up the sides of the cups.

Bake 50-60 minutes. A thin knife inserted in the center of the custard should come out clean when it is done. Serve warm or chill in the refrigerator.

*Variation:*

After custard is baked, fold in shredded coconut, sliced fruit, gorp, granola, or chopped nuts and seeds.

## • CRANBERRY-NUT PUDDING •
### 6 minutes   Serves 8

3 cups whole cranberry sauce
6 tablespoons softened butter
  or Butter's Brother (page
  14)
¼ cup honey

1 egg
½ cup unbleached flour
¼ teaspoon allspice
⅓ cup chopped walnuts

Preheat oven to 350°F.

Divide cranberry sauce evenly among 8 custard cups or oven-proof dishes. Set aside.

Combine butter and honey until fluffy. Beat in egg. Add flour and allspice and stir until blended. Fold in nuts.

Divide batter evenly among the cranberry-filled dishes. Place dishes on a baking sheet.

Bake 18-20 minutes. Serve immediately.

## • DATE CLOUDS •
### 6 minutes   Serves 4

1 cup whipping cream
1 tablespoon wheat germ
½ cup chopped walnuts
¼ cup honey

1 cup chopped dates
1 tablespoon orange or
  pineapple juice

Whip cream until stiff. Gently fold in remaining ingredients. Chill before serving.

## • GRAHAM CRACKER PUDDING •
15 minutes   Serves 4

This moist, fragrant snack is similar to a bread pudding. Serve it warm right out of the oven with ice cream, whipped cream, or fruit. Or enjoy it later sliced as a take-along treat.

**3 eggs, separated**
**½ cup honey**
**1 cup graham cracker crumbs**
  **(see Graham Scram**
  **Cookies, page 94)**

**½ teaspoon baking powder**
**1 teaspoon vanilla extract**

Preheat oven to 350°F.
   Beat egg yolks until thick and lemon-colored. Add honey, graham cracker crumbs, and baking powder, and mix thoroughly. Stir in vanilla.
   Beat egg whites until stiff. Fold into crumb mixture. Pour mixture into a buttered 1½-quart baking dish.
   Bake 30 minutes.

## • LEMON CURD •
10 minutes   Serves 4

**½ cup butter or Butter's**
  **Brother (page 14)**
**3 eggs**

**⅔ cup honey**
**½ cup lemon juice**

In top of a double boiler, melt butter.
   Beat eggs until light. Add eggs and honey to melted butter. Stirring constantly, cook over simmering water for 5 minutes. Add lemon juice and cook 3 minutes more until mixture is thick and smooth. Chill before serving.

*Variation:*

LEMON MERINGUE PIE—Plop Lemon Curd into a baked 9-inch pie shell. Top with meringue (page 119) and bake in a 425°F. oven for about 5 minutes or until meringue is lightly browned.


## • COOKED RICE PUDDING •
### 5 minutes   Serves 4

A great way to use leftover rice.

**2 cups cooked brown rice**
**1¼ cups milk**
**¼ cup honey**

**1 tablespoon vanilla extract**
**¼ cup raisins**

Combine all ingredients in a saucepan. Cook over low heat, uncovered, for 20 minutes. Stir occasionally. Cool and serve.

*Variations:*

Add sliced fruit—apples and peaches are especially tasty.

Add nuts, seeds, and granola.

Add dates or other dried fruit in addition to, or instead of, raisins.

Add ½ cup of grated raw carrot for added nutrients and a wonderful gold color.

## • RAISIN-RICE PUDDING •

6 minutes · Serves 6

3 cups milk
2 eggs
3 tablespoons honey
½ teaspoon nutmeg

2 tablespoons uncooked
  brown rice
½ cup raisins (optional)

Preheat oven to 300°F.

Scald milk.

While milk is heating, combine eggs, honey, and nutmeg. Slowly stir egg mixture into hot milk, stirring constantly
until blended. Add rice and raisins, if desired; stir well after each
addition.

Pour pudding into a 1½-quart baking dish. Set dish in a larger
pan and pour in hot water until it reaches the level of the pudding.

Bake 60 minutes. Stir occasionally while cooking. Serve warm
or cold.

# · Creamy and Crunchy Confections ·

We have a sneaking suspicion that this may be your children's favorite chapter in *S.N.A.C.K.S.*

The following confections are guaranteed to satisfy the most demanding sweet tooth. We're sure you'll want to try some of these recipes immediately, they sound so good. You won't be disappointed. On the contrary, it will be hard to believe something so satisfyingly sweet can actually be good for your kids. We don't advocate a steady diet of these treats, as tempting as they are, but every once in a while they are just the thing to surprise everyone with.

Follow the recipes carefully and measure accurately.

## Some Tips

Use a large enough saucepan so that candy (and honey) can cook freely without boiling over.

Watch the temperature carefully; it rises rapidly, especially after it reaches 220°.

There is great diversity among candies and how they should be handled. Different types of candies must be stored according to their ingredients. Although most candies can be kept in an airtight container, there are some exceptions. For example, candies made with noninstant dry milk should be refrigerated. Nut and seed mixtures may be stored in an airtight container in the refrigerator up to several weeks. Look for the specific storage directions at the end of each recipe.

## Freezing Candies

Many candies can be frozen for 6-12 months. Not all freeze well, however. Some may crack, split, or discolor. Be sure to wrap candies tightly in aluminum foil or plastic wrap.

Nut and seed mixtures may be frozen up to 2 months. If necessary, place them in a preheated 350°F. oven for about 5 minutes to restore crispness.

To thaw candies, allow them to stand at room temperature. Remove wrapping only after candy has thawed completely.

## • BAKED APPLES •
### 3 minutes

**For each serving:**

**1 apple**                                          **Cinnamon**
**Honey**
**Butter or Butter's Brother**
  **(page 14)**

Preheat oven to 350°F.

Core apples and scoop out a well. Don't cut through the apple completely. Fill well with honey. Dot with butter and sprinkle a little cinnamon on top.

Place apples in shallow baking pan with enough boiling water to cover the bottom of the pan.

Bake 40-45 minutes, or until apples are tender. Serve warm.

Store leftovers in the refrigerator.

## • CANDIED APPLES •
5 minutes

**For each serving:**

**Honey**
**1 apple**

**Shredded coconut, finely
chopped nuts, sesame
seeds, toasted wheat germ**

Place honey in a saucepan. Bring to a boil over medium-high heat and cook for several minutes. Remove from heat.

Insert a wood popsicle stick into each apple. Then dip the apple into honey and allow the excess to drip off.

Roll apple in one of the remaining ingredients.

If you are not handing candied apples out as fast as you make them, you can place them on wax paper or a greased cookie sheet.

*Note:* For a faster, kid-do-able candied apple, see No-Cook Candied Apples (page 27) in Quick and Easy section.

## • DRIED APPLES •
5 minutes   2 cups

Dried apples make great take-along treats. It is also possible to substitute them for fresh apples in your favorite apple pie recipe.

It is important to slice apples into uniform thin pieces. A food processor can be invaluable for this, especially if you want to double or triple the quantity, but it is not an essential.

Chunk 5 to 6 apples into at least 8 slices each but do not peel.

Place slices on a cookie sheet and *do not* allow them to touch one another. Place them in a 110-115°F. oven and leave for at least 6 hours or overnight, turning slices twice. Dried fruit should be dry on the outside but still soft inside with no moisture when squeezed.

Place apples in a loosely covered container. For the next five days condition apples daily by pouring them from one bowl to another several times to mix.

Store in an airtight container when thoroughly dried. They will keep up to 3 weeks.

## • BUGS •
10 minutes   2 dozen

½ cup honey                                    ¼ cup maple syrup

Boil ingredients in a saucepan until temperature reaches 260°F. on a candy thermometer, or until hard-ball stage.

Drop hot syrup onto a buttered cookie sheet to form quarter-size candies. Allow to cool and harden.

Store in an airtight container.

*Variation:*
Mix in ¼-½ cup of your favorite nuts and seeds.

## • CAROB-PEANUT QUICKIES •
10 minutes   4 dozen

¾ cup honey                    ½ cup Butter's Brother (page
½ cup carob powder                 14)
½ cup milk                     3 cups rolled oats
1 teaspoon vanilla extract     1 cup peanuts

In a saucepan, combine the first 5 ingredients and bring mixture to a boil over medium heat. Continue cooking and stirring constantly for 5 minutes.

Remove from heat and add oats and peanuts. Mix well.

Drop mixture by teaspoonfuls onto wax paper and allow to cool.

Store in an airtight container and refrigerate.

## • CRUNCHY CARROT NUGGETS •
### 10 minutes    2 dozen

¼ cup cream cheese
½ cup shredded Cheddar cheese
1 teaspoon honey
1 cup finely grated carrot

⅓ cup chopped nuts or sunflower seeds
2 tablespoons finely chopped parsley

Blend the first 3 ingredients until smooth. Stir in grated carrot. Cover and chill mixture ½ hour.

Roll mixture into balls about 1 inch in diameter. Store in the refrigerator until ready to serve.

Combine chopped nuts or seeds and parsley. Just before serving, roll balls in this mix and completely coat.

Store leftovers in a covered container and refrigerate.

## • CURRY CORN •
### 4 minutes    2 quarts

2 quarts popped popcorn (about ½ cup pre-popped)
1 cup nuts

2 tablespoons butter or Butter's Brother (page 14)
1 teaspoon curry powder

Put popcorn in a large bowl. Add nuts and toss.

Melt butter in a saucepan until it begins to bubble. Add curry powder and stir. Drizzle curry/butter over popcorn and nuts and toss until evenly glazed.

Store in an airtight container.

## • DATE SUPREME CANDY •
12 minutes    2 dozen

½ cup water
½ teaspoon cinnamon
4-5 cups (about 2 pounds)
  pitted dates, loosely packed

Shredded coconut, granola,
  crushed peanuts,
  sesame or sunflower
  seeds, or wheat germ
Whole almonds

Bring water to a boil in a saucepan. Add cinnamon. Drop in dates and cover pan with a tight-fitting lid. After 1½-2 minutes, turn heat off and allow mixture to sit for about 5 minutes, or until it is soft.

Blend date mixture until it is creamy. Shape small amounts into balls when it is cool enough to handle. Roll each ball in remaining ingredients and top with an almond.

Store in an airtight container. May be refrigerated.

*Variation:*
  Mix date mixture with peanut butter before rolling into balls.

## • FABULOUS FUDGE •
5 minutes    1½ pounds

This may just turn out to be your favorite snack recipe. It's a fast, sure hit—even with diehard junk-food fans. We make it in a saucepan to help melt the honey and peanut butter, but you can mix it right in the serving pan.

1 cup peanut butter
1 cup honey

1 cup carob powder

Put peanut butter and honey in a saucepan and heat slightly, stirring occasionally until mixture blends easily. Add carob powder and stir well.

Put mixture into a greased 8-inch square pan and flatten into the corners. Cool and store in the refrigerator. Cut into squares before serving.

*Variation:*

Add shredded coconut, dates, chopped nuts, raisins, sesame seeds, sunflower seeds, or wheat germ to the basic recipe after adding carob powder.

## • FRUIT LEATHERS •
10 minutes

These need no refrigeration and keep for months.

Choose either fresh (be sure to peel and chunk it) or canned (drain well) fruit. Some good choices are apple, peach, or pear.

Cover a cookie sheet with plastic wrap.

Blend fruit until it is a fine puree. Spread puree as thinly as possible on plastic wrap, making sure there are no holes and that puree does not touch edges.

Set oven at lowest possible temperature (150°F.). Leave cookie sheet in oven overnight, or until puree is dry and leathery. Roll up leather and plastic wrap. Tear off pieces whenever the kids want a snack.

## • HONEY-BAKED BANANAS •
2 minutes

**For each serving:**

Peel 1 banana and place in a greased baking pan. Brush with honey until banana is entirely covered.

Bake at 350°F. for 15-20 minutes, or until banana is fork-tender. Serve immediately.

Spread mixture on a greased cookie sheet.
Bake 20-30 minutes, stirring after the first 15 minutes.
Store in an airtight container.

*Variations:*
Add roasted soybeans or chopped dried fruit.
For toddlers, blend or grind granola until it is very fine. Serve soaked in milk.

## • GRANOLA •
10 minutes    5 cups

**2 cups rolled oats**
**½ cup shredded coconut**
**½ cup chopped nuts**
**½ cup bran or wheat germ**
**½ cup sesame seeds**

**½ cup sunflower seeds**
**¼ cup honey, warmed**
**¼ cup vegetable oil**
**¼ teaspoon vanilla extract**

Preheat oven to 350°F.
Mix the first 6 ingredients in a large bowl. Drizzle honey, oil, and vanilla over dry ingredients and toss to mix well.

## • JELLY BELLYS •
10 minutes    3 dozen

**4 envelopes (4 tablespoons)**
  **unflavored gelatin**
**1¼ cups cold water**

**¾ cup frozen apple juice**
  **concentrate, thawed**

In a medium-size saucepan, sprinkle gelatin over water. Stir over moderately low heat, about 5 minutes, until gelatin is completely dissolved. Remove from heat and stir in juice concentrate.
Pour mixture into an 8-inch square pan and refrigerate 2 hours or more until firm. Cut into squares.
Store covered in the refrigerator up to several days.

## • MAPLE NUTS •
10 minutes    2 cups

½ cup maple syrup
1 tablespoon cinnamon
1 tablespoon butter or Butter's
  Brother (page 14)

1½ teaspoons vanilla extract
2 cups walnuts

In a skillet, combine the first 3 ingredients. Cook and stir over medium heat until mixture becomes brown and starts to thicken. Add vanilla and stir. Add nuts and toss until they are evenly coated with glaze. Cool on wax paper.

Eat as candy or serve over cake, ice cream, or fruit.

Store in an airtight container in the refrigerator.

## • NUTS AND BOLTS •
7 minutes    4 cups

¼ cup butter or Butter's
  Brother (page 14)
2 teaspoons tamari sauce
1 cup whole rice cereal

1 cup whole wheat cereal
1 cup thin pretzel sticks
½ cup peanuts

Preheat oven to 250°F.

Melt butter in a saucepan over medium heat. Stir in tamari sauce.

In a large flat baking pan, combine the remaining ingredients. Slowly pour butter mixture over cereal/nut mixture. Stir until evenly coated.

Bake 60 minutes, stirring every 15 minutes. Remove from oven and cool thoroughly before storing in an airtight container.

Variation:

Add popcorn to mixture after it is prepared.

## • POPCORN BALLS •
### 15 minutes   1-1½ dozen

Be careful not to touch popcorn mixture until it has cooled.

**2 quarts popped popcorn**            **½ cup honey**
  **(about ½ cup pre-popped)**

Put popcorn in a large bowl.

Bring honey to a boil over low heat and let simmer for 10 minutes.

Pour cooked honey over popcorn and gently toss with buttered forks until popcorn is evenly coated. Butter your hands and press handfuls of coated popcorn into balls and place on wax paper.

Store in an airtight container.

## • RAISIN-NUT CLUSTERS •
### 12 minutes   3-4 dozen

**¼ cup molasses**            **2 cups peanuts**
**1 teaspoon cider vinegar**      **1 cup raisins**
**½ cup honey**
**3 tablespoons butter or**
  **Butter's Brother (page 14)**

In a saucepan, combine the first 3 ingredients. Cook over low heat until mixture reaches 260°F. on a candy thermometer or the hard-ball stage. Remove from heat.

Add remaining ingredients in the order listed. Stir well after each one. Drop mixture by teaspoonfuls onto wax paper or greased baking sheet.

Store in an airtight container.

## • SAVORY SUNFLOWER SEEDS •
10 minutes   1 cup

1 tablespoon butter or Butter's
   Brother (page 14)
1 teaspoon vegetable oil

1 cup sunflower seeds
1 teaspoon chopped chives
½ teaspoon garlic powder

In a small skillet, heat butter and oil over low heat. Add sunflower seeds, chives, and garlic powder. Stir well. Toast about 8 minutes, shaking and stirring occasionally. Serve immediately or store in an airtight container and refrigerate.

## • SESAME-NUT CANDY •
15 minutes   3-4 dozen

½ cup peanut butter
½ cup honey

1¾ cups granola
1 cup sesame seeds

Mix the first 3 ingredients until smooth. Chill mixture for 10 minutes in the refrigerator.

As mixture is chilling, put sesame seeds in a large skillet and heat over moderate heat about 5 minutes, shaking and stirring until they are golden brown. Place seeds on wax paper and cool.

Form mixture into balls—about 1 inch in diameter—and roll each ball in sesame seeds until it is well coated.

Store in a single layer in a covered container in refrigerator.

## • SNACKER-JACKS •
15 minutes   2 quarts

Our version of a popular commercial product.

**2 quarts popped popcorn**              **1½ cups peanuts**
  **(about ½ cup pre-popped)**            **¾ cup honey**

In a large bowl, mix popcorn and peanuts.

Bring honey to a boil in a small saucepan. Let simmer over low heat for 10 minutes. Pour honey over popcorn/nut mixture. Toss with buttered forks or spoons until evenly coated.

Store in an airtight container.

## • TOFFEE •
15 minutes   ¾ pound

**¼ cup chopped nuts**                   **½ cup honey**
**½ cup butter**

Butter an 8-inch square pan. Sprinkle nuts in pan.

Melt butter in a saucepan over medium heat. Gradually add honey, stirring occasionally to prevent it from burning. Cook 5-7 minutes, or until honey is golden brown. Pour over nuts in pan and allow to cool before marking candy into 1-inch squares with a knife. When completely cool, break into pieces along marked lines.

Store in an airtight container and refrigerate.

# · Freezer Friends ·

"A friend in need is a friend indeed," so the old adage goes. No one is more in need at times than a parent trying to come up with a quick and nutritious snack idea.

These cool and refreshing snacks are indeed friends, ready and waiting to please your children and requiring little preparation time from you.

Most of these recipes make fairly large amounts, at least enough to serve 4 children, and often more. Others can be easily expanded to meet your needs. In any case, these delicious frosty treats will disappear quickly, so be prepared. You know how we feel about double batches, and extras can always wait their turn in the freezer up to 3 months.

## Some Tips

Store ice cream in the coldest part of the freezer. Keep containers tightly sealed to prevent loss of flavor and ice crystals from forming.

For the best flavor, allow ice cream to soften at room temperature for about 15 minutes before serving.

Try not to use a wet spoon to remove ice cream from the container. The drops of water will cause ice crystals to form when the ice cream is replaced in the freezer.

## • ALMOST FUDGICLES •
5 minutes   Serves 6

½ cup water
¼ cup vegetable oil
¼ cup honey

1 teaspoon vanilla extract
½ cup carob powder
3 shelled hard-boiled eggs

Blend the first 4 ingredients in blender until smooth. Add carob powder and eggs and blend until smooth. Spoon mixture into popsicle molds or paper cups and insert a wood stick as a handle.
Freeze until hard.

## • LIQUID GOLD CREAMSICLES •
5 minutes   Serves 4-6

Make Liquid Gold drink on page 65, according to the directions.
Pour mixture into paper cups or plastic popsicle molds and freeze.
Serve when hard.

## • FROZEN FRUIT YOGURT POPS •
5 minutes   Serves 6

1 cup strawberries
1 cup plain yogurt

⅓ cup honey

Blend berries until smooth. Add remaining ingredients and stir with a spoon until mixture is blended. Pour mixture into paper cups. Put a wood popsicle stick into the center of mixture to use as a handle. Freeze until firm. Remove from cup to serve. (Yogurt mixture may also be poured into plastic popsicle molds.)

## • ICE MILK •
### 6 minutes   Serves 6-8

4 eggs
1 cup milk
1 banana, chunked or 1 cup
  berries

1½ teaspoons vanilla extract
¼ cup vegetable oil
2 tablespoons honey
2 cups heavy cream

Beat the first 3 ingredients until smooth. Add vanilla, oil, and honey, and blend. Add cream and continue to blend until mixture is smooth. Pour into popsicle molds or paper cups and freeze until firm.

*Variation:*
For fluffier ice milk, pour the mixture into a large container and allow to freeze slightly. Remove from freezer, beat well, and return to freezer until firm.

## • ELSIE'S LEMON ICE •
### 10 minutes   Serves 6

1½ cups honey
4 cups boiling water
¾ cup fresh lemon juice
  (include pulp)

1 tablespoon grated lemon
  peel

Stir honey and boiling water in a bowl until honey is dissolved. Allow mixture to cool slightly. Add juice and lemon peel and stir well.

Freeze mixture until it is mushy. Beat with an electric mixer, and return to freezer to harden.

## • CREAMY FRUITY FROZEN MOUSSE •
5 minutes   Serves 4

**1 cup whipping cream
1 can undiluted frozen grape
  juice concentrate, thawed**

Whip cream until it is stiff.
  Blend in frozen juice concentrate. Place mixture in freezer and allow to harden. Garnish with blueberries, if desired.

*Variation:*
  Try other juice flavors; apple, lemonade, and orange are some good choices.

## • FESTIVE PEANUT FREEZE •
8 minutes   Serves 6

**¾ cup cream cheese
½ cup mayonnaise
3 tablespoons lemon juice
½ cup crushed pineapple,
  drained**

**2 bananas, chunked
¼ cup chopped grapes
½ cup chopped peanuts
1 cup cream, whipped**

Blend the first 3 ingredients until creamy and smooth. Stir in fruit and peanuts. Fold in whipped cream. Pour mixture into a cold loaf pan or freezing tray. Return to freezer until mixture is firm.
  Slice and serve. Garnish with peanuts, if desired.

## • STRAWBERRY ICE CREAM •
### 10 minutes   Serves 6

1½ cups milk
1½ tablespoons unbleached
  flour

½ cup honey
1 cup cream, whipped
1¼ cups strawberries, mashed

On top of a double boiler, blend milk and flour. Add honey and cook until mixture is thick. Pour into a 1-quart pan or plastic container and place in the freezer.

When mixture begins to freeze, fold in whipped cream. Stir in strawberries and return to freezer to harden. Stir occasionally.

## • TUTTI-FRUTTI ICE CREAM •
### 6 minutes   Serves 6

4 tablespoons raw cashews
4 tablespoons noninstant dry
  milk
2 cups pineapple juice
4 tablespoons (heaping) frozen
  orange juice concentrate,
  thawed

1 cup chunked banana, fresh
  or frozen
1 cup drained pineapple
  chunks

Blend the first 3 ingredients until smooth. Add orange juice concentrate and blend. Stir in fruit. Pour mixture into a 1-quart plastic container or individual paper cups and place in the freezer to harden.

## • VANILLA ICE CREAM •
15 minutes    Serves 6

1 cup honey
2 cups heavy cream
2 cups milk

1 tablespoon vanilla extract
3 eggs, separated

Mix the first 3 ingredients in a saucepan and cook, stirring constantly, until mixture begins to boil. Remove from heat.

Stir in vanilla. Set pan in a bowl of ice water and stir occasionally.

While cream mixture is cooling, beat egg yolks until frothy and beat egg whites into soft peaks.

Pour the cream mixture into egg yolks and stir. Gently fold in egg whites. Pour mixture into a 1-quart plastic container and freeze until firm.

*Variation:*
If you desire, before ice cream has hardened, stir in fruit and/or nuts of your choice.

## • WALNUT ICE CREAM •
7 minutes    Serves 6

1 cup maple syrup
1 cup water
3 egg whites

2 cups cream, whipped
1 cup chopped walnuts

In a saucepan, boil the first 2 ingredients for 1 minute. Remove from heat.

Beat egg whites until stiff. Add to the cooled maple syrup/water mixture. Fold in whipped cream and walnuts. Pour mixture into a 1-quart plastic container and freeze. Stir occasionally while freezing.

# · Incredible Spreadables ·

Our incredible spreadables—butters, dips, and spreads—made with cheese, fruit, and nuts can't be considered snacks in themselves. But, oh, the wonderful snacks that can be made when these foods are served with quick and whole grain breads, biscuits, crackers, fruit, ice cream, muffins, pancakes, and vegetables. Any one of these foods can be enhanced nutritionally, deliciously, and quickly by these spreadables.

Make them when you have a few extra minutes, place in a covered container in the refrigerator or, for longer storage, in the freezer. They will always be on hand when you need a healthy snack in a hurry.

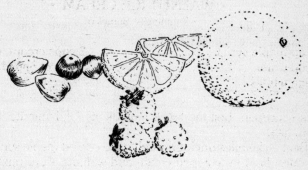

## • CHEESE-NUT BALL •
6 minutes   3 cups

1 cup chopped peanuts,
  divided
1 cup Cheddar cheese
¼ cup blue cheese

¾ cup cream cheese
¼ cup finely chopped onions
¼ cup finely chopped parsley
1½ cups tamari sauce

Save ½ cup peanuts.
  Beat all ingredients until mixture is smooth and blended. Chill.
  Shape mixture into a ball and roll in the remaining ½ cup of chopped peanuts.
  Store in the refrigerator wrapped in plastic wrap or aluminum foil.

*Variation:*
  Substitute walnuts for peanuts.

## • DAPPLE BUTTER •
6 minutes   1½ cups

1 apple, chunked
½ cup apple or pineapple juice

10 large dates, chunked
½ cup sunflower seeds

Blend chunked apple and juice. Add dates, a few pieces at a time, and continue blending until mixture is smooth and thick. Stir in seeds.
  Good with apples, bananas, and almost any breads.
  Store in the refrigerator.

*Variation:*
  Heat over a double boiler if you prefer it warm.

## • GEE WHIZ •
15 minutes   2 cups

Our version of a popular but additive-loaded cheese spread.

You may use many types of cheese in this recipe, but Cheddar is our favorite. Its tangy sharpness lends a distinctive flavor that goes well with crackers or bread when used as a sandwich spread. It can also be reheated in a double boiler and used as a sauce or fondue while still warm.

| | |
|---|---|
| 2 tablespoons butter or Butter's Brother (page 14) | 1 cup milk |
| 2 tablespoons unbleached flour | 1 cup grated Cheddar cheese |
| | 1 egg, slightly beaten |
| | Pepper to taste |

Melt butter in a saucepan over medium heat. Remove pan from heat and blend in flour. Return to heat and slowly add milk, stirring constantly until smooth and slightly thickened. Add grated cheese and continue stirring until completely melted. Stir in egg and pepper. Remove from heat and cool.

Store in a covered container and refrigerate.

## • ORANGE MARMALADE •
8 minutes   1½ cups

Not only is this delectable treat a natural on whole wheat toast, it is also super on hot pancakes, nut breads, and rolls, or spread between the layers of a cake. You will always want to keep a jar stashed away in the refrigerator.

| | |
|---|---|
| ½ cup honey | 2 orange rinds |
| 1 orange, peeled and chopped | |

Blend all ingredients in blender or food processor until mixture is smooth and blended.

## • HONEY BUTTER •
5 minutes    1 cup

½ cup butter or Butter's
  Brother (page 14) softened
½ cup honey

¼ teaspoon cinnamon
¼ teaspoon nutmeg

Blend all ingredients until butter is fluffy and thoroughly mixed with other ingredients.

Serve on whole wheat toast or biscuits, or melt and serve over pancakes.

Store in a covered container in the refrigerator.

*Variation:*

Combine crushed pineapple, strawberries, grated orange peel, and cinnamon and add to honey butter.

## • ORANGE-HONEY BUTTER •
5 minutes    1 cup

½ cup butter or Butter's
  Brother (page 14)
⅓ cup honey

2 tablespoons frozen orange
  juice concentrate, thawed

Blend all ingredients until mixture is light and fluffy.

Store in a covered container and refrigerate.

## • PEACH BUTTER •
### 5 minutes   1½ cups

**1 16-ounce can peaches,**
  **drained**

**½ cup honey**
**¼-½ teaspoon cinnamon**

Blend peaches to a smooth puree. Stir in honey and cinnamon until blended.

Store in a covered container in the refrigerator.

## • PINEAPPLE BUTTER •
### 5 minutes   1 cup

Use the juice from the canned pineapple.

**2 cups pineapple chunks,**
  **packed in their own juice**
**2 apples, chunked**

**Pineapple juice**
**Honey**

Blend pineapple chunks and apple chunks. Add enough pineapple juice to make a thick butter. Stir in honey to taste.

Store in a covered container and refrigerate.

## • INSTANT PINEAPPLE SAUCE •
### 6 minutes   2 cups

**1 20-ounce can pineapple
chunks, packed in their
own juice**

Drain pineapple chunks.
   Blend pineapple until it is well blended and smooth.
   Place mixture in a saucepan and heat over low heat until just
warm. Serve over cake, fruit, or ice cream.
   Store in a covered container and refrigerate.

## • STRAWBERRY JAM •
### 15 minutes   4 cups

Frozen whole strawberries may be used.

**4 cups fresh strawberries,
   washed and hulled
½ cup honey**

**1 tablespoon lemon juice
2 tablespoons water**

Combine all ingredients in a saucepan, crushing berries slightly
as you stir. Bring mixture to a boil, stirring constantly, and continue boiling as it thickens. Jam is done when candy thermometer
reads 240°F., or when jam falls in a thick mass from the spoon.
   Pour jam into clean jars and allow to cool.
   Store in the refrigerator.

## • WALNUT-HONEY SPREAD •

6 minutes   1 cup

1½ cups walnuts
3 tablespoons vegetable oil,
  divided

2 tablespoons honey

Blend walnuts in a blender or food processor until they are slightly ground.

Add 1 tablespoon of oil and blend. Scrape down the sides of bowl with a rubber spatula.

Add another tablespoon of oil. Blend and scrape.

Add the last tablespoon of oil; then add the honey. Blend and scrape. Mixture will be smooth and creamy. Spread on breads, crackers, or fruit.

Store in a covered container in the refrigerator.

## • YOGURT CREAM CHEESE •

You can make a delicious creamy "cheese" from yogurt. Whether it is homemade or a commercial brand of plain yogurt, this rich solid can be used in many recipes in place of sour cream, ricotta, or cottage cheese.

Wrap 1 cup of yogurt in cheesecloth several layers thick. Hang cheesecloth bag containing yogurt from the kitchen sink faucet and allow it to drip in the sink for 12-24 hours. Unwrap molded cheese and store in a covered container in the refrigerator.

*Variations:*

Mix with cinnamon, ground cloves, or nutmeg for a quick topping to serve with fruit or cake.

Thin with a little lemon or orange juice for a unique, quick sauce.

# · Maxi Snacks ·

At first glance, Maxi Snacks may appear to contain an eclectic collection of recipes, but all are substantial enough to be served as a meal or, at the very least, as a hearty, filling snack that will hold older children and young adults until mealtime.

Soups, sandwiches, pancakes, and pizza make great snacks, and you'll be surprised at how quickly you can make them.

Because so many of our Maxi Snacks are soups and sandwiches, we have included some tips on how to store, freeze, and brown-bag them.

## Some Tips

Many soups and sandwiches can be stored in the refrigerator for up to a week. For longer storage, freeze.

When packing sandwiches that are to be eaten later, store them on their edges, instead of flat, to prevent them from becoming soggy.

Freeze sliced meat sandwiches ahead of time for brown-bag lunches. They will be thawed by lunchtime but still fresh and cold.

Wrap lettuce leaves separately when packing sandwiches for lunches. The kids can add them to the sandwich just before eating and they will remain much crisper.

165

To make sandwiches for a crowd, use an ice cream scoop to portion out the fillings accurately and effortlessly.

Cut-outs are designs cut out of the center of slices of bread and then used as sandwich tops. A simple circle, triangle, smile, or star can enchant a young child.

Catch a child's fancy by cutting a face out of a slice of cheese. Cut out the eyes, nose, and mouth and place on the sandwich filling. (You can broil it if you prefer.)

Mugs are easier for small hands to hold and they can help prevent spills. Somehow soup sipped from a mug is more fun too.

Thermos-packed soups are a nourishing school lunch or snack. Try popped popcorn as a garnish for soup. Kids love it!

## Freezing Soups and Sandwiches

Heavily waxed cartons or plastic containers are perfect for freezing soups. Leave a 1-inch head space for expansion.

Soups can be frozen up to 6 months.

Before freezing sandwiches, tightly wrap them individually in aluminum foil, plastic wrap, or plastic bags, and label clearly.

Put sandwiches in a single layer until they are frozen, then stack them.

If you plan to freeze sandwiches, omit the following ingredients and add them *after* the sandwiches have thawed: fruit butters, hard-boiled eggs, lettuce, mayonnaise, and tomatoes.

Pack frozen sandwiches for school lunches. They will be thawed but still refreshing by lunchtime.

Sandwiches can be frozen up to 1 month.

## • APPLE FRITTERS •
### 10 minutes   1 dozen

1 cup unbleached flour
1½ teaspoons baking powder
1 egg
3 tablespoons honey

5 tablespoons milk
2 unpeeled apples, thinly sliced

Whisk flour and baking powder. Make a well in the center. Add egg, honey, and milk, and blend well.

Gently fold sliced apples into batter and coat thoroughly. Remove apples from batter with a tablespoon and fry in hot, oiled skillet until golden brown. Flip and cook the other side. Allow fritters to drain before eating.

*Variation:*
BANANA FRITTERS—Use 3 bananas, chunked, instead of apples.

## • APPLESAUCE •
10 minutes    Serves 6

**8 medium-size apples,**                    **½ cup water**
   **chunked**

Put apples and water in saucepan. Cover and bring to a boil. Turn down heat and simmer 15-20 minutes, or until apples are tender. Remove from heat.

If desired, add about ¼ cup of honey and/or 1 teaspoon of cinnamon.

Serve warm or cold.

## • BUSY BAKEQUICK PANCAKES •
10 minutes    8 pancakes

**2 cups Busy Bakequick**                    **2½ cups milk**
   **(page 20)**                            **1 egg**
**⅓ cup vegetable oil**

Mix all ingredients thoroughly. Pour batter onto a hot, lightly oiled skillet or griddle. When the pancakes are golden brown, flip them and cook the other side for a few more minutes.

Serve immediately.

*Variations:*
For thicker pancakes, use only 1½-1¾ cups of milk.
Add a handful of bran or wheat germ to batter for extra nutrients.

## • BUSY BAKEQUICK WAFFLES •
7 minutes    4 waffles

2 cups Busy Bakequick
  (page 20)
3 tablespoons vegetable oil

1¾ cups milk
1 egg

Mix all ingredients thoroughly. Cook batter on a preheated waffle iron until golden brown.

## • CHEESE BURGERS •
10 minutes    Serves 4

2 cups shredded semi-hard
  cheese (our choices are
  Muenster or Monterey Jack
  cheese)
4 tablespoons butter or
  Butter's Brother (page 14),
  softened

1 cup dry bread crumbs
1 tablespoon chopped parsley
  (optional)
2 teaspoons Dijon mustard
¼ teaspoon pepper
2 eggs, well-beaten

Blend all ingredients thoroughly. Shape mixture into 4 patties.
  Sauté patties in vegetable oil over low heat until browned on both sides. Serve immediately with your children's favorite condiments.

## • CHEESE FRITTERS •
10 minutes    2 dozen

These light, crispy puffs are so delicious you will have everyone begging for more. We don't recommend using a blender or food processor; an electric mixer or that miracle of human anatomy, the hand, works fine. Another nice thing about this recipe is that it can be made hours ahead of time and yet the total time spent actually preparing and cooking it is under 15 minutes.

**2 eggs**
**1 cup ricotta cheese**
**⅓ cup unbleached flour**
**1½ tablespoons butter or**
  **Butter's Brother (page 14),**
  **softened**

**1½ teaspoons grated lemon**
  **peel**
**Vegetable oil**

Beat eggs lightly in a bowl. Add cheese and blend well. Slowly beat in the flour. Add butter and lemon peel and continue to blend.

Cover the batter and refrigerate it about 2 hours. Remove from the refrigerator about ½ hour before cooking to allow it to reach room temperature.

In a large saucepan, measure oil to ½-inch depth and heat to 375°F. Drop batter by large spoonfuls into the hot oil.

Fry until golden brown and puffy, turning over once.

Drain on paper toweling. Serve warm with honey drizzled over them.

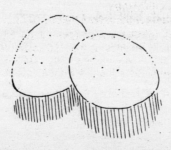

## • CHEESE RAP •
10 minutes   Serves 4

¼ cup butter
1 egg
1 egg white
2 tablespoons milk
4 slices raisin bread

¼ cup cream cheese, softened
1 apple, cut into quarters
1 tablespoon honey
½ teaspoon lemon juice
Cinnamon (optional)

Preheat oven to 450°F.

In a preheated 13 x 9-inch pan, melt butter until bubbly. Remove from oven and spread butter evenly.

Beat 1 egg and 1 egg white with milk in a shallow dish. Dip bread slices in egg mixture until both sides are well coated. Place bread in buttered pan. Bake for 5 minutes. Remove from oven.

While bread is baking, beat cream cheese until fluffy. Cut each apple quarter into 4 slices. Combine honey and lemon juice and toss with apples.

Turn bread slices over in pan and spread each slice with cream cheese. Top with apple slices and return to oven.

Bake 5 minutes, or until cheese is set and apples are tender. Serve immediately. If desired, sprinkle with cinnamon.


## • TOASTED CHEESE ROLL-UPS •
10 minutes   Serves 4

¼ cup cream cheese, softened
1 tablespoon butter
½ teaspoon chopped parsley

Dash of pepper
4 slices thin whole wheat
 bread

Preheat oven to 350°F.

Blend the first 4 ingredients until smooth. Spread mixture on bread slices and carefully roll up the slices. Secure with toothpicks and place on a greased cookie sheet.

Bake 8-10 minutes. Remove toothpicks and serve immediately.

*Variations:*
Sprinkle grated Cheddar cheese on roll-ups and pop back into the oven for the last couple of minutes of baking time.
Spread a thin layer of your favorite jam or nut butter over the cream cheese mixture before rolling up.

## • ENERGY PIES •
10 minutes   8 pies

These are great anytime of the day, but we especially like them for a get-up-and-go breakfast. And we do mean "go"! These are very portable snacks. Make them up ahead of time and freeze for an even smoother start on those busy A.M.s.

**Pastry for an 8- or 9-inch pie**

**½ cup mashed banana**
**⅓ cup peanut butter (we like to use the chunky kind)**

**⅓ cup dates, chunked**
**1 tablespoon honey**

Preheat oven to 375°F.
Roll pastry out on a lightly floured surface to a rectangular shape. Cut into 8 triangular pieces. Cut each triangle in half.
Blend the remaining ingredients until smooth. Spoon mixture onto 8 of the triangles of dough. *Don't get it too close to the edges.* Moisten each triangle's edges with water. Then cover with another triangle of dough. Press edges together with a fork to seal. Pierce top with a fork's tines several times. Place on a cookie sheet.
Bake 12-15 minutes. Cool.

## • FRUIT COBBLER •
### 7 minutes   Serves 6

This quick snack can be served warm or cold. It is nutritious enough to enjoy at breakfast.

1½ cups chunked apple
½ cup unbleached flour
½ cup rolled oats
2 tablespoons honey

3 tablespoons butter or
    Butter's Brother (page 14),
    softened
Dash of cinnamon

Preheat oven to 350°F.
  Place chunked fruit in a buttered baking dish. Combine the remaining ingredients until mixture is crumbly. Spread over fruit.
  Bake 20-25 minutes, or until brown and bubbly. Cool slightly before serving, or store in the refrigerator for future snacks.

## • FRESH FRUIT FACE •
### 8 minutes   Serves 4

Kids love to make their own fruit faces. They have as much fun eating them as they do making them.

1 cantaloupe, cut into 4
    1-inch thick circles
1½ cups cottage cheese
2 tablespoons raisins
1 tablespoon sunflower seeds
Dash of cinnamon

4 cups mixed fresh fruit
    (include grapes or cherries
    and banana plus apples,
    blueberries, peaches, pears,
    pineapples, plums, or
    strawberries)

Place cantaloupe circles on lettuce-lined plates.
  Combine cottage cheese, raisins, and sunflower seeds with cinnamon. Spoon this mixture into the center of the cantaloupe circles. Surround with mixed fruit.

Let the kids make a face on the cottage cheese, using grapes or cherries for eyes, a cherry for a nose, and a banana, sliced in half, lengthwise, for a mouth. Serve immediately.

## • GAZPACHO •
10 minutes    Serves 4

A satisfying lunch or supper for those summer days when it is too hot to cook.

2½ cups vegetable juice
2 medium tomatoes, chopped
¾ cup chopped cucumber
¾ cup chopped celery
¼ cup chopped green pepper
¼ cup chopped onion

¼ cup chopped parsley
1 garlic clove, minced
2 tablespoons lemon juice
Dash of Tabasco sauce
   (optional)

Combine all ingredients and chill 2-4 hours. Serve cold.

## • MARVELOUS MACARONI SOUP •
10 minutes    Serves 4

4 cups unsalted bouillon
2 cups cooked elbow
   macaroni (or 1 cup dry
   elbow macaroni cooked in
   boiling water and drained)

1½ tablespoons butter or
   Butter's Brother (page 14),
   melted
2 tablespoons grated
   Parmesan cheese
2 tablespoons minced parsley

Heat bouillon to boiling.

In a pan or bowl, toss macaroni with butter, cheese, and parsley. Pour in the boiling bouillon and stir once or twice.

Serve with more Parmesan cheese sprinkled on top.

## • MELON BOWL AMBROSIA •
### 15 minutes    Serves 4

2 medium-size cantaloupes
1 cup pineapple chunks
1 cup strawberries
¼ cup coconut, divided

1 frozen banana, chunked
½ cup plain yogurt
½ teaspoon nutmeg
1 tablespoon lemon juice

Cut cantaloupes in half. For a more attractive edge, use a zigzag cut. Remove seeds and scoop out meat. Set aside ¾ cup of meat.

Combine the remaining cantaloupe meat, pineapple chunks, strawberries, and 2 tablespoons of coconut. Spoon this mixture into cantaloupe halves.

Blend the ¾ cup of cantaloupe meat in a blender or food processor until it is smooth. Add chunked frozen banana and blend until mixture is smooth. Add remaining ingredients and blend again. Spoon this sauce over fruit. Garnish with remaining coconut. Serve immediately.

## • MINUTE MINI PIZZAS •
### 10 minutes    Serves 2

1 English muffin, cut in half
   and toasted
Grated Parmesan cheese

1-2 tablespoons tomato sauce
2 slices mozzarella cheese
⅛ teaspoon oregano

Sprinkle grated Parmesan cheese on each muffin half. Spoon tomato sauce over cheese, making sure to spread it to the edges of the muffin. Cover each half with a slice of mozzarella cheese and sprinkle oregano on top.

Place pizzas as far away from broiling unit as possible and broil until cheese is melted and bubbly, sauce is hot, and muffin is warm throughout. Serve immediately.

## • PEACH MELBA •
12 minutes    Serves 4

For a real treat, try this when peaches are in season and cheap and plentiful. Allow 1 peach, pitted and cut in half, per serving.

**½ cup raspberries, fresh or frozen but thawed**
**1 teaspoon honey**
**Dash of cinnamon**
**¼ cup ricotta cheese or ½ cup plain yogurt**

**1 16-ounce can unsweetened peach halves, packed in their own juice**

Blend raspberries until they are liquefied.
Blend in honey. Stir in cinnamon and set aside.
If using ricotta cheese, beat it until it is fluffy. Fill the centers of the peach halves with cheese or with yogurt. Spoon raspberry sauce over filled peaches and serve immediately.

## • PICK-UP STICKS •
### 15 minutes   2 dozen

These are well worth a little extra work. They have a slightly sweet flavor and are a perfect portable snack as well as a nice change at mealtime.

| | |
|---|---|
| **1 tablespoon active dry yeast** | **½ cup boiling water** |
| **½ cup very warm water** | **1 egg** |
| **2 tablespoons honey, divided** | **3 cups unbleached flour** |
| **½ cup butter or Butter's** | **½ teaspoon water** |
| **Brother (page 14), melted** | **Sesame seeds** |

Sprinkle yeast over warm water in a small bowl. Stir in 1 teaspoon of honey and let stand until mixture is bubbly, about 8 minutes.

Meanwhile, mix the rest of the honey, butter, and boiling water in a large bowl and set aside.

Beat egg and reserve 1 tablespoon. Stir remaining egg into butter mixture. Add yeast water and blend well. Stir in flour to form a soft dough.

Divide dough into 24 equal parts. On a floured surface, roll each piece into a stick shape about 6 inches long. Place on a greased cookie sheet, about 2 inches apart.

Mix reserved egg with ½ teaspoon of water. Brush on bread sticks and sprinkle with sesame seeds. Let stand for 30 minutes.

Preheat oven to 425°F. Bake 15 minutes.

## • PIZZA PIE •
10 minutes
2 pizzas    Serves 6-8

*Mama mia!* This is good pizza!

**2 cups Busy Bakequick**          **⅔ cup milk**
**(page 20)**                      **¼ cup vegetable oil**

Preheat oven to 375°F.

In a large bowl, combine all the ingredients. Stir until mixture leaves the sides of the bowl. Using your hands, gather dough and form a ball. Knead it 10 times in the bowl. Divide dough in half.

On a lightly floured surface, roll each half out to form a 12-inch circle. Place each circle on an ungreased cookie sheet. Turn up edges by pinching the dough.

Spread 2 tablespoons of oil on each circle and then sprinkle on the following ingredients in the order listed. These amounts should be divided between the two pizzas.

**¾ cup grated Parmesan**          **1 teaspoon dried oregano**
**cheese**                         **¼ teaspoon pepper**
**1 cup tomato sauce**             **1 cup shredded mozzarella**
**2 tablespoons chopped onion**    **cheese**

If pizza isn't pizza without such goodies as mushrooms, anchovies, etc., add these just before the mozzarella cheese.

Bake 20-25 minutes. Serve hot.

Unbaked pizza can be placed in the freezer until it is hard. Remove, wrap in aluminum foil, and mark clearly. Return to freezer and store up to 2 months.

## • PICKLED EGGS •
10 minutes    6 eggs

Use within 2 days of preparing.

¾ cup beet juice (drained from
  a can of beets)
¾ cup cider vinegar
¼ cup honey

12 whole cloves
6 eggs, hard-boiled and
  shelled

Mix the first 4 ingredients in a saucepan. Bring mixture to a boil. Cool.

Place eggs in a quart jar. Pour in beet juice mixture and cover. Refrigerate overnight.

## • PRETZELS •
15 minutes    1½ dozen

With just a little practice, this is a quick and easy treat to make. Double this recipe and freeze the extras.

1 teaspoon active dry yeast
1 cup unbleached flour
1 cup whole wheat flour
1½ teaspoons honey

1½ cups warm water
1 egg
Coarse salt (optional)

Preheat oven to 450°F.

In a large bowl, place yeast, flours, and honey. Add water and mix until the dough forms a ball. Small amounts of flour can be added, if necessary.

On a well-floured surface, knead dough until it is smooth and elastic—about 5 minutes. Pull off small pieces of dough, and, using your palms, roll each piece on the floured surface or between your hands to form thin rods about 8 inches long. Shape each rod into a pretzel shape. Using a fork dipped in cold water, mash ends slightly into center to seal and hold shape.

Using a spatula, place pretzels on a lightly oiled cookie sheet.

Beat the egg slightly and brush it on pretzels. Sprinkle with coarse salt, if desired.

Bake 12 minutes, or until lightly browned.

## • RAG-TAG SOUP •
15 minutes    Serves 4

4 unsalted bouillon cubes
4 cups boiling water
4 tablespoons grated
  Parmesan cheese

1 cup bread crumbs,
  preferably fresh
2 eggs, slightly beaten

Place bouillon cubes and boiling water in saucepan and bring to a second boil. Allow bouillon to dissolve.

Mix remaining ingredients. Gradually add this mixture to boiling bouillon, stirring constantly for 10 minutes.

Serve topped with more grated Parmesan cheese.

Store leftover soup in the refrigerator.

## • RICOTTA PUFFS •
7 minutes    2 dozen

1 cup ricotta cheese
1 egg
½ teaspoon grated onion

24 whole wheat bread rounds
¼ teaspoon paprika

Beat cheese and egg until blended. Add onion and beat again.

Toast bread rounds on one side. Heap cheese/egg mixture on the other side and broil 1 minute, or until cheese is puffy. Sprinkle with paprika and serve hot.

*Variations:*

Omit onion and add ½ cup of Parmesan cheese and 1 tablespoon of chopped parsley.

Omit onion and add ½ teaspoon of orange peel, ¼ teaspoon of cinnamon, and 1 teaspoon of honey. Sprinkle with cinnamon or finely chopped nuts.

Use slices of whole grain or (better yet) raisin bread instead of bread rounds. Either cut into quarters or serve as open-faced sandwiches to older children.

## • SIMPLE SWISS SOUP •

8 minutes    Serves 4

½ cup butter or Butter's
  Brother (page 14)
½ cup unbleached flour
2½ cups boiling water

Dash of pepper
Dash of nutmeg
1 cup grated Swiss cheese

In a saucepan, blend butter and flour over medium heat, stirring constantly, until mixture is golden and bubbly but not brown.

Add boiling water, pepper, and nutmeg, and stir until mixture is smooth. Simmer for ½ hour.

Just before serving, add cheese and blend well. Serve immediately.

*Variations:*

Use boiling bouillon instead of water.

Remove soup from the stove and stir in 1 beaten egg yolk just before serving.

## • SUMMERTIME STRAWBERRY SOUP •
10 minutes    Serves 4

2 cups strawberries, sliced,
  divided
1 cup apple or orange juice
3 tablespoons lemon juice

2 tablespoons unbleached
  flour
Honey (optional)
1 cup plain yogurt, divided

Blend 1½ cups strawberries with apple or orange juice until a puree is formed. Pour mixture into a saucepan and place over low heat.

Meanwhile dissolve flour in lemon juice. Add to strawberry mixture and cook about 5 minutes, or until mixture thickens. Remove from heat. If desired, add honey to taste at this time.

Fold remaining strawberries and ¾ cup yogurt into soup mixture. Refrigerate until soup is well chilled, at least 2 hours. Garnish with a dollop of yogurt before serving.

## • FRENCH TOAST-WICH •
10 minutes

For each serving:

2 eggs, beaten
1 tablespoon milk
1 teaspoon honey
1 tablespoon peanut butter

2 slices whole wheat bread
1 tablespoon butter or Butter's
  Brother (page 14)

Beat eggs and milk until blended. Add honey to peanut butter and blend. Spread mixture on 1 slice of bread. Top with the other slice.

Dip sandwich in egg mixture, coating both sides.

Sauté in butter over medium heat until golden brown. Flip and cook the other side. Serve immediately.

*Variations:*
Add a dash of cinnamon to egg mixture.

Substitute a slice of mozzarella or Muenster cheese for the peanut butter filling. Dip sandwich in egg mixture and sauté as directed above.

Spread tuna salad on bread to make a sandwich. Dip in egg mixture and sauté as directed above. For a real protein plus, add a slice of cheese before sautéing.

## • ZUCCA SNACKS •

10 minutes    2 dozen large squares

¾ cup unbleached flour
1½ teaspoons baking powder
2 tablespoons chopped onion
Dash of pepper
½ cup grated Parmesan
  cheese

4 eggs
½ cup vegetable oil
3 cups zucchini, cut into thin
  slices

Preheat oven to 350°F.

In a large bowl, combine the first 5 ingredients and mix lightly.

Blend together eggs and oil. Stir mixture into the flour mixture, using a fork to blend smoothly. Fold in zucchini. Spread batter evenly in a buttered 13 x 9-inch pan.

Bake 40 minutes, or until squares are lightly browned. Cool slightly before cutting into squares.

Serve warm or store in an airtight container.

# · Lists of Lists ·

When you quickly need an idea or two for a fast, healthy snack or dessert, look no further. We have compiled some of the many recipes in *S.N.A.C.K.S.* that we feel will help you and have listed them under different headings for easy and quick reference. We hope they will be of some help when you are in a pinch for time and inspiration.

## Feeding the Gang

## Holiday Hits

## Have Snack, Will Travel

## School's Out

## Party Favors

| | Page | | Page |
|---|---|---|---|
| Natural Fruit Soda | 37 | Coconut Cake | 110 |
| Orangeade | 37 | Devil's Food Cake | 111 |
| Ice Cream Balls | 31 | Curry Corn | 143 |
| Spicy Popcorn | 54 | Fabulous Fudge | 144 |
| Carob Brownies | 89 | Creamy Fruity Frozen | |
| Cheese Twists | 90 | Mousse | 154 |
| Corn Chips | 91 | Strawberry Ice Cream | 155 |
| Whole Wheat Crackers | 103 | Vanilla Ice Cream | 156 |
| Favorite Basic Cake | 108 | | |

## Lazy Hazy Days

| | Page | | Page |
|---|---|---|---|
| Banana Pom Poms | 39 | Continental Cheesecake | |
| Frozen Banana | 40 | Pie | 130 |
| Just Juice Cubes | 40 | Lemon Curd | 135 |
| Pudding-on-a-Stick | 41 | Jelly Bellys | 146 |
| Yogurt Fruit Delight | 41 | Almost Fudgicles | 152 |
| Mild Tuna Medley | 43 | Elsie's Lemon Ice | 153 |
| Instant Italian Ice | 51 | Fruit Cobbler | 172 |
| Pineapple Sherbet | 52 | Gazpacho | 173 |
| Cucumber Cooler | 62 | Melon Bowl Ambrosia | 174 |
| Fancy Dancy Lemonade | 65 | Pickled Eggs | 178 |
| Watermelon Whoopee | 68 | Summertime Strawberry | |
| Best Blueberry Muffins | 72 | Soup | 181 |
| One-Pan Apple Cake | 106 | | |

## Breakfast Specials

| | Page | | Page |
|---|---|---|---|
| Branola Cereal Snack | 28 | Cran-Apple Drink | 62 |
| Mellow Yellows | 33 | Florida Fantastic | 63 |
| British Banana Sandwich | 43 | Jim's Instant Breakfast | 64 |
| O.G.'s Bonnet Eggs | 50 | Banana Orange Bread | 72 |
| Golden Grapefruit | 51 | Popovers | 80 |

## Breakfast Specials

## Just Desserts

## Baby Bonanza

# · Index ·

187

℗